# HIG
## at Hacienda del Diablo

By

# ALEX CORD

**Based on a story by Jerry Nalls**

*This book is for all my compadres in Texas*

# Acknowledgements

I owe so much to so many people who have influenced my life. I could easily fill many pages with names. Regarding this book, there are several who have hovered while I covered blank pages with words. *HIGH MOON* would not exist without the tenacious insistence and continuing support of the intrepid Nick Wale. The idea for the story was inspired by an original story by Jerry Nalls.

Westerns have been an integral part of my life from as far back as I can remember anything. It started with the Lone Ranger serials on Saturday afternoons. The price of admission was 5 cents, a nickel. I was riveted. It was also on the radio, Monday, Wednesday and Friday nights. I sat on the floor with my head plastered to the speaker. The radio was the size of a Volkswagen.

I am grateful to dear friend, Bo Hopkins, for his thoughtful foreword. Thanks to Kevin Diamond for the super cover. Over the years I've had the privilege of working with some of the greats, Kirk Douglas, Ernest Borgnine, Sam Peckinpah, Robert Fuller, Van Heflin, George C. Scott, Ben Johnson, Slim Pickins, Bing Crosby, Buck Taylor, Wilford Brimley, Barry Corbin.

Gary Cooper, Larry McMurtry, Louis L'Amour, Zane Grey, Clint Eastwood, Joel McCrea, John Wayne, Walter Brennan, Audie Murphy, Robert Mitchum, Burt Lancaster, James Stewart, and countless others have all made deep lasting impressions on Alex Cord. I have been blessed and I thank God for the gifts I've received.

# A Note From Bo Hopkins

Alex Cord and I have known each other since we were whippersnappers. He would bring his son, Damien, who was in puppyhood, to my house to join a swarm of kids to flounder around in my pool. Damien left us far too soon to go to heaven. It left a wound in Alex that will never heal. I admired him and respected his talent as an actor. I believe it was mutual and the foundation for a bond that still endures, in spite of the tyranny of geography. We never worked together but both had the unique experience of working with Sam Peckinpah in different films. It has been a great source of pleasure for me to see Alex become a successful and respected writer.

His gripping novel, "A Feather in the Rain" won the Glyph Award for Best Popular Fiction. He has played polo with Prince Charles. He knows horses inside and out. He has roped steers with Ben Johnson and Larry Mahan. He has owned a ranch in Texas for fifteen years. He's a consummate story teller and has now turned his hand to a Western.

As you are about to find out, "HIGH MOON" is a fast paced classic told in a unique style. The characters are fully realized. They leap from the page and stand in front of you sweating. You can hear them, smell them and know how you feel about each one.

The good guys are truly heroic individuals with human flaws. Brantly Stormer is a man I hope to hear a lot more about. The villains do not help old ladies to cross the street. They are relentless in their violent lack of morality. Alex, with his knowledge of horses and ranching, brings the life and times of lawless, south Texas and the Mexican border to flesh and blood life...and death. It's a story of savage brutality, redemption and the discovery of a profound love. Once started, you will be swept along on a non-stop gallop through the old west.

Alex is a dear friend and I am proud to have had this opportunity to offer my thoughts about him and his captivating gift as a writer.

## 1

It was a shriek of pure joy that drifted through the swirling dust. The stallion, mane flying, ducked his head between his forelegs and thrust his hind feet high in the air, his hooves clacked together. He gathered himself and galloped away bucking and kicking. The woman stood hands on hips laughing. She flapped her arms to urge him on. He got to the fence, stopped and turned to face her. He shook his head, rared up pawing the air, screamed again and charged forward along the fence of the large pen. She stepped forward in a playful threat. He continued to circle her as fast as he could run and still keep his feet under him.

Totally aware of his magnificence, he broke to a trot tossing his luxuriant mane and tail. All four feet left the ground simultaneously as he shot straight up in the air and came to earth in a full gallop. He was the epitome of the majestic breed called the Andalusian. Even through the Texas dust there was a metallic gleam to his lion-colored coat. In sharp contrast, the abundance of mane and tail were black, as was the dorsal stripe from mane to tail. His legs from above the knees and hocks on down to his hooves were black. He was an astonishing sight as he trotted up to Amanda Lawson and poked his flaring nostrils at her. She rubbed his face gently, glowing with love and enchantment at the wonder of him. She put her arm over his neck, kissed his cheek and began to walk in an aimless manner. He dropped his head and followed like a pet hound.

Sir Lionel Lawson was a British expatriate, to the manner born. He grew up as landed gentry. A gifted horseman, he played polo with Royalty and "rode to the hounds" pursuing the fox. His beloved wife, Camilla, had succumbed to an illness which took her to heaven, leaving him devastated, to raise their daughter, Amanda. A ravishing, dark beauty with purple eyes, she was always a bold adventurer who put the boys to shame. It was not intentional but there often seemed to be an element of scorn perceived by the young men in her life. She fell close to the tree and gave her father the reason to go on.

Sir Lionel had always harbored an obsessive interest in the American West and the cowboys who played such a huge part in the development of the cattle industry.

He came home from a long, dreamed-of-visit to America with a new passion for life. His love for his wife was so complete and the loss so overwhelming as to leave no room for any desire to seek a relationship with another woman. His daughter was everything to him. He shared his enthusiasm for America with her and discussed the possibility of moving there. Her predictable life had become tiresome. She yearned for adventure and leaped at the idea. "I can become a Texas cowgirl, learn to rope and shoot a six-gun. Yeehah!"

And so he bought the land in Texas and developed Quail Run Ranch. Together they built a flourishing enterprise with a focus on breeding good horses and cattle.

Apart from her natural and learned skills with horses, Amanda had a special gift. An affinity with all animals, an ability to communicate with them beyond the normal kinship that many folks have. She could talk to them and listen to their responses. It was a thing that was obvious to Sir Lionel and the few who witnessed it, if they had the will to believe.

# 2

Sir Lionel had committed totally to being an American Texan though he'd not taken to saying, "y'all." Though sensitive to the comfort of his neighbors and the ingrained culture of Texas, his inherent upbringing of such longstanding would not be denied. He employed servants and the table was set accordingly. Two dogs, an Australian Shepherd and a Blue Heeler curled together in a corner. They did not move. Senator Harley May and wife, Mattie sat to his right, Amanda, his left. Tom and Susan Hastings were neighbor ranchers. Tom, an eager horseman, wanted to know more about the new stallion.

Sir Lionel, keen to oblige, responded. "The Andalusian has been around since thousands of years before Christ. They were used primarily as war horses and to some extent still are. They are extraordinarily athletic and are now used to fight bulls in Portugal and Spain. They are called the horse of Kings. They have an intelligent and willing nature. With all due respect for the thoroughbred and the cow horse, I believe they can have a serious impact on the horse industry here. Amanda, tell Tom what you feel about Zarco."

She put her wine glass down flashing a luminescent smile and said, "In all my life with horses, I've never seen anything like this. He is utterly amazing. He can canter sideways on a loose rein, change leads with the slightest shift of weight in the saddle. If you are not perfectly balanced and in sync with him, you will soil your britches. Tom, he is phenomenal and an absolute love. He plays like a puppy but his power is awesome. One needs to stay awake around him. You've got to come and watch me work him. I promise you a treat."

Tom Hastings had a ton of respect for Amanda and her ability with horses. "Ah caint wait." He raised his glass. "Here's to the Andalusian." They all joined in the toast.

# 3

Tom Hastings and wife, Susan, sat with Lionel and his ranch foreman, Clayton Moore, at a viewing table under the shade of a thatched roof next to the pen. The dogs were flopped in the sand under the table. A pitcher of cold tea and glasses soothed parched throats. The sun had not yet reached its full-powered height. Their eyes were focused on Amanda riding the stallion, Zarco. She sat tall and straight as if she had grown out of his spine. His powerful neck arched as if restrained, but the reins were slack as he cantered a small circle with all his weight balanced on the hindquarters leaving his forelegs free to cross in a pirouette. Tom's jaw had fallen open as Lionel turned to look at his friend. Tom just shook his head slowly from side to side. Susan reached over and gently placed her hand under Tom's chin and lifted it shut.

"When will his wife arrive? Tom asked.

"In about a month's time." Lionel answered.

"From the same place in Brazil?"

"Yes sir."

"What color is she?"

"A blood bay."

Tom blew out a breath and shook his head, "What a pair that's gonna be."

"I am hoping it will be the birth of a dynasty."

"And they're good around cattle?"

"They're bred for it. I'll get Clayton to bring in a few cows and you can see for yourself."

# 4

The finger nail clip of a moon gave a pale cool light to the quiet night. An owl hooted. Three riders moved silently through the trees like shadows dripping river water. Two Mexicans, and one Comanche made their way like cats toward the compound of Quail Run Ranch. The dogs roused with a low rumble and made their way toward the approaching riders. Sir Lionel was by nature a trusting soul and in all his years in Texas had the good fortune to never have experienced any threat to his person or property. His dogs were not trained guard dogs and reacted to the strangers on pure protective instinct. The Comanche slipped from his saddle with a sack in hand and kindly offered generous hunks of beef to the two dogs. He hunkered down and was able to show an affection. In a matter of small minutes, he was stroking them. The two Mexicans rode well-trained horses right up to the pen where the stallion stood in the pallid light.

One stepped down handing his reins to the other. He held a rope in one hand and a halter over his shoulder. He went through the gate murmuring softly to Zarco. With only half a swing his loop sailed softly over Zarco's head with him barely noticing. The man gently took out the slack and approached the horse. He was a skilled horseman. He slipped the halter over the stallion's head, removed his catch rope and led Zarco out of the pen. He handed the lead rope to the other Mexican and mounted his horse coiling his rope. He took the lead rope from the other. They turned and walked away, shadows in the night. The Comanche came out of the trees and joined them. The entire event accomplished with extraordinary finesse took but a few minutes, while the ranch slept. The owl hooted.

Clayton Moore was a cowboy in every fiber of his self. He was raised on a ranch, became a top hand and took his work seriously. Cuz he loved it. He was average height, compact, with no fat. He'd tried marriage once and it didn't work. He'd been with Lionel since the start. He liked the Englishman and his unique manner of being. He respected him for his courage and intelligence. He'd never met a man like Sir Lionel. Clayton was a loyal, dependable friend. He held Amanda in the highest regard. He was always the first one up in the morning and the last one to bed at night. He climbed into his clothes and stepped out of the bunkhouse as the other hands were coming to life. Daylight was working its way from the east. Coffee was in the air as he made his way to the kitchen.

As he approached Zarco's pen and saw that it was empty, he glanced around. The gate was closed. He hastened back to the bunkhouse. Ricardo was in charge of the horses and just about to leave the bunkhouse as Clayton came in. "Ricardo, did you move the stallion from the pen?"

"No sir."

"He's not there." They both bolted out the door and ran to the barn.

Sir Lionel and Amanda joined Clayton, Ricardo and four cowboys at the pen gate taking care to avoid the tracks leading away. Clayton, young Trey Gowdy along with Buck Taylor and String Bean followed the tracks to the Rio Grande and paused where the thieves had crossed. They scanned the opposite bank and urged their horses into the water vigilant on what might be hidden waiting. Midway across, two quick shots rang out as Trey and Buck's horses were hit and went down in the river.

The Comanche watched as the four scrambled for Texas leaving two dead horses behind. He was a stinking, unwashed critter with a deep, wide scar that ran from the top of his forehead down through the sealed socket where an eye had been. A warrior had taken issue with his unwanted attention to his squaw and planted a tomahawk in his skull. He grinned at the floundering cowboys, lowered his rifle, slowly turned his horse and disappeared among the trees. His name was Mato, meaning bear.

♣

Amanda was so young she hardly remembered her mother, Camilla. She was profoundly affected by Zarco being taken and not knowing what would happen. She sat in shock while the men discussed what should be done. Clayton felt responsible as did Lionel. "How could I have been so idiotically naïve as to not have seen that he was better protected?" He put his arm around Amanda in apology and an effort at comfort. She seemed to be unaware of the gesture.

"Our options are quite limited, aren't they? He's in bloody Mexico isn't he. Manuel Rojas has him and he's got an army to help him keep him. Hasn't he? We do not have an army. We are not bandits and gunfighters. What do we do?" Lionel looked from one man to another. Each was silent. "I understand. We cannot go charging into the jaws of death in another country with no legal right, no evidence. Clayton, what do we know about Rojas?"

"He fancies himself a general. Most of his gang think of him as a general. He's a two-bit murderer, the son of a murderer. His father was a killer bandit who lay in wait for innocent peasants to rob and kill. He ended with his head blown off by a shot gun in the hands of one who had enough. His two brothers were killed by gun dealers. Rojas has managed to survive in his fortified hacienda with his band of cut- throats protecting him."

"What does he want with this horse?"

"He is known as a fine horseman. He has an unusual love for horses. Somehow he has had knowledge of your horse."

"Do you think I could buy the horse back from him?"

"He would take your money, give you the horse and then steal him back again. He is not someone to make a deal with."

Amanda seemed to rouse from her shock and said, "Could we hire our own gunfighters to get Zarco back?"

The silence was thick. Finally, after some minutes passed, Clayton spoke with some hesitance. "Many years back I was in the middle of a sticky situation that involved an extraordinary man. His name was Brantly Stormer. I was able to do him a favor that he might remember. If I could ever find him again. He was a Texas Ranger of some reputation, then he disappeared, retired. He was an extremely capable individual. I've heard a rumor that he was somewhere up near Campobello."

"Well let's get him here. Talk to him." Lionel was ready to move on anything that sounded hopeful.

"That would never happen. We'd have to try to find him and see if he would even talk to us."

# 5

Hacienda El Diablo was a Spanish fortress surround by high white walls manned by armed guards. A fat-bellied, dirty, guard carrying a rifle called from the wall to a balcony. "General, they have the horse for you to see."

Manuel Rojas stepped out from the hacienda and looked down. The three thieves stood proudly by the bathed and groomed stallion. Gleaming in the sun, burnished bronze with black frills, Zarco was a sight to behold.

Rojas smiled wide and flung his arms to the sky. "Eiyee, Dios Mio! In a few years we will have the best horses in all of Mexico." A woman appeared at his side. He put his arm around her and cupped her partially exposed breast. "Is he not the most exquisite hombre?"

"Si, muy guapo." She hauled him back into the hacienda as they led Zarco away. She was an intelligent woman who paid attention to what Rojas was up to. She knew that knowledge was power and the more knowledge she had the better off she'd be. Once inside she said, "What if his former owner decides he wants him back?"

"Then he can come and try to take him."

"But he will not dare." Encarnita was not timid.

"Someone will come." Rojas seemed pleased with that possibility and dismissive. "Let us have some wine to celebrate this treasure of a horse."

♣

Campobello was a small town Northeast of the Rio Grande with a saloon, one whore and a place to eat. Clayton had been there but not for a spell. He and Sir Lionel rode down the main street toward a blacksmith banging on the red-hot start of a horse shoe. Clayton said, "Afternoon." The smith plunged the iron into a bucket of water and over the hiss said, "Howdy."

"Wonder if you might be able to tell us where we'd find Brantly Stormer."

"Wonder if you might tell me why you want to find him."

"Got some business we'd like to discuss with him."

As if they'd not spoken, the blacksmith went back to shaping the shoe at his forge. Lionel turned to Clayton. "Perhaps we'd best see to this matter on our own." Clayton said, "Thank you, sir," and turned his horse up the street. They tied up in front of the saloon where a man was sweeping dirt and dead flies into the street. They stepped up onto the walk. Lionel said, "Good afternoon, sir. I presume you are open for business."

"If Ahm here Ahm open for business."

"Excellent. Two whiskeys will do." They walked into the place and up to the bar.

Bartender Malcolm said, "Comin' up." He moved behind the bar, brought out a bottle and two glasses and started to pour. "Thank you," said Lionel. "Do you mind if I ask your name?"

"Malcolm."

"Malcolm. That's a fine name. Don't hear that every day. Malcolm would you happen to know a Mr. Brantly Stormer?"

Malcom came on guard. "Mind if Ah ask why you want to know?"

"No. We have some business we'd like to discuss with him. Personal business."

Malcolm moved on down the bar to serve another customer. Lionel and Clayton heard a metallic click behind them and a low rasping voice say, "You two fellas keep real still. One at a time with your left hands put your guns on the bar and push 'em away from you."

They did as told. "Now slowly, turn around."

Brantly Stormer was six foot four and hard as steel. His hat was low over his eyes in their permanent squint. He had a five-day growth of unshaven hair and a long barreled pistol levelled at Clayton and Lionel.

"I'm listenin."

"Mr. Stormer, I presume."

"What do you want?"

Lionel looked to Clayton. "Would you do the honors?"

Clayton stepped forward, with ease. "My name is Moore, Clayton Moore. I'm foreman of the Quail Run Ranch. This here is Sir Lionel Lawson; he owns the ranch. He would like to talk to you about hirin you."

"Me or my gun?"

"I figured they go together."

"He ain't got enough money."

Lionel stepped forward. "Perhaps I could surprise you."

"What I'm saying is, enough money doesn't exist. Anywhere." He turned and left.

Lionel followed Stormer out while Clayton gathered their guns and walked out behind Lionel. Stormer, at his horse, snugged his cinch and stepped lightly into the saddle. His horse was a finely made chestnut mare with a flaxen mane and tale. She looked to have some thoroughbred in her. There was the aura of speed about her. He looked down at Clayton. "Moore, Clayton Moore. Seems I know you from somewhere."

"I gave you a hand once in Bandera. Long time ago."

Stormer nodded as the memory came to him. "The day we hung Cooter Crockett. You took his brother's gun away from him when he was fixin to shoot me. Had you not been so quick, he'd a put a bullet in me. You figure I owe you?"

"No sir. You said 'thanks' at the time."

"Well, I'll say it again, 'thanks'."

"Mr. Stormer, will you just let me explain?"

"No."

"We've had a long and dusty ride. May I ask why you won't even talk to us?"

"You've got nothin' I want."

"Whatever your price is, I'm prepared to pay it."

"I've already told you about money."

"There must be something you desire."

"Nothin' money can buy."

"It's been my experience, money can buy almost anything."

Stormer shifted in his saddle and leaned closer to Lionel. He'd made a decision to enlighten the man. "Almost," he said. "Can't buy back years of bad choices. Dead men's lives. A girl I should've married. The kids I might've had. There's a lot money can't buy." He lifted his reins lightly, turned his horse and rode away. Lionel was left deep in thought. Clayton handed him his pistol. "Looks like we come a long way for nothing."

Lionel holstered his gun. "See to the horses, will you, Clayton? I'll fix us some rooms for tonight."

Brantly Stormer's reputation was born out of accomplishments and nourished by the truth of his deeds. His reputation had acquired a life of its own almost as something apart from the man. And yet they were inextricably linked, as long as he remained alive. His rep stood there as a glaring challenge like a mountain daring to be climbed. Anyone could attempt it but it wasn't free. You had to put up your life.

Not long past sunrise, it was already blazing hot as Lionel and Clayton walked down the street to Suli's Café. Several horses were tied at the rack in front. As they stepped up on to the walk, Clayton noticed a particular horse and said, "That's Stormer's mare."

"So it is."

Suli's Café was neat and clean. Among the customers were a banker and his client, a Drummer and his sample case on the floor beside his chair, a young drifter and at the rear, together at the same table, the blacksmith and Brantly Stormer. Lionel and Clayton found a vacant table and sat with a brief glance in Stormer's direction. Though their eyes met for a second, Stormer gave no indication of acknowledging their presence.

Suli was big bosomed and well fed with a huge warm smile. She carried two plates of steaming breakfast and set them down in front of Brantly and Bill, blacksmith. "There you go. Now Ah wanna be able to see my face in those plates when y'all finish."

She moved on to check on the banker and his client and then to the young drifter. "Everthaing all right, young man?"

"Yesum." He was tight-faced and serious.

"You holler if you need anythin."

He managed a nod as she crossed over to Sir Lionel and Clayton. "Coffee, gents?"

Lionel said, "If you please."

Suli reacted to his accent and moved to the counter for the coffee pot. As she poured, she asked, "Where y'all from?"

A twinkle formed in Lionel's eye, "Just a little south of here." He exaggerated his accent with a smile.

"Everbody a little south of here talk lahk thet?" Suli said. Clayton laughed.

Lionel with mock awareness said, "Oh, you mean originally?"

Suli attempted a Texas version of a British accent. "As a matter of fact, I do!"

Lionel appreciated Suli's sense of humor. "Lancashire, my dear. Lancashire, Great Britain." They all laughed.

"What can Ah get y'all?"

As they ordered breakfast, the young drifter was focused intently on Brantly Stormer. Suli approached his table. Without looking at her, he said, "What do I owe yuh?"

She glanced at his empty plate. "Two bits."

He dropped a coin on the table and stood. He'd kept his hat on all the while. He adjusted his gun belt, took a deep breath and moved over to the table where Brantly and Bill were eating. Brantly immediately coiled. He squinted up from under his hat brim.

"Brantly Stormer?"

Brantly remained silent, looking straight at the young man who was rigid with hate. "Like to be sure. Hate to kill the wrong man."

Bill placed his fork on the table and moved back out of the way. In an instant, the entire café was aware. The banker and client stood and fled. Lionel and Clayton froze. The drifter stepped back and readied himself. Brantly slowly placed his napkin on the table. His eyes never left the young man. "Don't do this, son."

"Anytime, ol' man." He stood consumed by a boiling rage of hatred.

"Back off. If you don't, you will die."

"You first."

Brantly sighed in resignation, adjusted his napkin on the table and slowly stood up. "All right. But not in here. Outside."

"The only way you're gettin out of here, is feet first." The young fool made his move. Before he could even clear his holster, Brantly had drawn his forty-four, cocked and jammed it into the drifter's belly. His gun never left the holster. As he realized he was a hair away from death, beads of sweat popped out and covered his face. The world stopped breathing. Nothing moved.

Brantly's voice was almost a whisper. "Let it slide back in the holster. Real careful."

The sweating man eased his fingers and let the uncocked gun down into the holster. His knees began to shake as a wet spot appeared below his belt buckle.

"Left hand. Open the buckle and ease the gun belt to the floor."

As he did, Brantly raised his gun and placed the muzzle against the drifter's upper lip, under his nose. "You can leave now."

Barely able to stand, he wobbled out the door.

Brantly holstered his gun and sat back down as Bill returned to his chair and reached in his pocket for money. Brantly stopped him with, "It's on me. Cuz of me your breakfast was disturbed."

The sound of the front door being kicked open was followed by the young drifter with a rifle pointed at Brantly. He fired as Brantly shot him right between his eyes. He flew backwards out the door into the street.

The mess had been cleared. Suli had a basin of water, alcohol and bandages and was tending to Brantly's wounded arm. It was a superficial grazing. "How in the name of heaven were you able to shoot him that quick when he came in blasting?"

"I was expectin him. I'm gonna have to get your door fixed."

Sir Lionel and Clayton were out on the street, in shock at what they'd witnessed. "I believe I might have something that could be of interest to Mr. Stormer. More than money. Will you be kind enough to get our horses while I see if I can get a word with him?"

At a corner table in Suli's café, Brantly signed a paper and handed it back to Sir Lionel. He read it. "Excellent. I'll expect you in two days. Yes, and by the way, that is a very fine mare you're riding. What do you call her?"

"Tree Fightin Woman."

♣

Didn't matter which way they turned to look, there was nothing but vast open plains parched in every direction under the blue prairie sky. They were going back the same way they'd come so they were prepared for the long dusty ride. Lionel was optimistic. "It turns out that nothing aggravates Mr. Stormer as much as does a horse thief. He and I share the same passion for good horses. That and the fact that I offered him two hundred fifty acres of prime land up in that isolated high country and the materials to build a house, plus the assurance that no one would know he was there was the thing that got him to sign on. He's a curious fellow."

Clayton corked his canteen. "He is surely acquainted with a passel of odd individuals from politicians to cutthroats."

"I believe he could gather quite an assemblage of capable chaps."

# 6

A building smaller than the bunkhouse held extra tack, odd equipment, several bunks and a pot-bellied stove. Gathered were Lionel, Clayton, Brantly Stormer and an older man with a white mustache and steel blue eyes as keen as a falcon. He was known as Digger Carlson. A longtime friend of Brantly's from way back. A man of varied persuasions and skills. He'd been a mountain man in the Rockies, a sharp-shooter in a Wild West Show and a bank-robber who never got caught. Brantly had described him as "the best shot I've ever seen with a rifle. There's not a nerve in his body." He came by the name, Digger, when he was a young boy. Six renegades had raided his home and killed his mother and sister while he and his dad were out mending fences. He alone tracked them down, charged into their camp and killed them all. He lined up their bodies side by side, pulled his knife and carved a cross on the forehead of each. Then left them to the scavengers of the plains. He became a man of solitude and spent most of his life alone following whatever paths beckoned.

"We need to find out everything we can about Rojas's fortress. Determine what supplies we need to get the horse back and make sure Rojas will not be coming to get him again. Simple as that," Brantly declared.

"We do know they've got him in a fort and they're not going to bring him out to us." Lionel stood and paced slowly.

Brantly, through the smoke from his nostrils, said, "When faced with a resistant task, I've often favored the principal of 'a bigger hammer'."

Clayton asked, "Meaning?"

"We start with dynamite. I've been thinking about a man who for years worked in the mining business as an explosives expert. He might be persuaded to participate in our noble cause. If I can find him."

♣

The Cougar Gap Trading Post was the closest thing to a town not far from Lionel's ranch. It was a gathering place for those who had no other and for those passing through. One might see a neighbor or someone from parts unknown. The main building housed a general store with everything for ranch and farm. A barber's chair and a saloon were combined with a place to eat. Brantly had tracked down Humphrey "Stick" Comstock and was armed with a shopping list from the dynamite man by way of telegraph. He was only about 100 miles away setting on his porch with a jug of whiskey watching a herd of goats. His wife had died of fever a few years back. His daughter lived twenty miles away with her husband and little girl. Humphrey, who'd been known most of his life as "Stick," was a thready, pale-haired man surrounded with an atmosphere of having just been insulted. He compensated with a wild, raucous laugh that erupted unexpectedly without apparent cause. He'd consented to join Brantly's band.

Wilford Bryan wore steel-rimmed glasses on a round nose above a walrus mustache. He didn't know Brantly Stormer but realized he was with Sir Lionel and Clayton. Lionel introduced them and Brantly handed him his list. Wilford looked over the list and nodded. "Three cases of dynamite. Looks like you're planning on relocating some solid material." He looked over the top of his spectacles at Brantly, silent. Then shifted his gaze to Sir Lionel. "That is a possibility. We have a wagon out front, if you would be so kind while we have something to eat."

"I will see to it, Sir Lionel." Wilford smiled at the small pleasure he took from his use of the aristocratic title. Lionel turned to him and spoke softly, "Wilford, I appreciate your kindness in using the formal, Sir, but I'm a little embarrassed by it here in Texas, so if you wouldn't mind, I'd prefer you call me Lionel."

Wilford laughed and said, "Lionel it is. Here in Texas I could call you Mr. Lionel and that wouldn't raise any hair."

"Fine."

They moved toward the dining area. "Just set wherever you like. I'll be right with you."

There were about ten or more folks of every description at tables. Clayton ever the watch dog, scanned the room and paused for a brief nod to a young Mexican man in a far corner. He was called Juanito Torres. He wore patched clothes and packed a good six-gun at his side. He rose from his seat and walked slowly across the room to the table where Sir Lionel, Brantly, Digger Carlson, and Clayton sat.

He stood stiffly, removed his hat and said, "Mr. Clayton." He nodded in greeting.

"Juanito." Clayton stood, shook his hand and introduced them all. Juanito possessed a refined, confident, manner in contrast to his humble appearance. He looked directly at Sir Lionel.

"Señor, it is a very unfortunate thing what has happened with your horse."

Lionel and his group were immediately attentive. "What do you know of it?" Lionel asked.

"I know he was stolen from your rancho by the men from General Rojas. I know where they have him."

"Have you seen him?" Lionel was on his feet in front of Juanito. He nodded yes. "How is he?"

"He is fine. He is being cared for well. Rojas knows about horses. The horse is at his hacienda."

"Why do you tell me this? What do you want?"

"I want to ride with the men you will be sending."

"Who are you?"

"I am Juanito Torres."

Wilford Bryan was pouring drinks and listening to the conversation.

Lionel said, "How do you know this information? Why do you want to help? How do we know you don't work for Rojas?"

Wilford said, "I can vouch for that."

Brantly said, "You know this man?"

"I know he has no love for Rojas. Show these men your neck, Juanito."

Juanito unwrapped a scarf from around his neck and revealed a thick, lumpy scar. Wilford continued, "One of Rojas's men did a clumsy job of cutting his throat there."

"I would like to return the favor. But I will not be so clumsy."

Brantly walked around the table and stood towering over the young man. He glared down at Juanito who met his cold eyes with a steady, patience. "We are going to bring back a horse not to help you seek revenge."

"Señor, if you do not kill Rojas, you will have no success. I have seen him and his Comancheros rape and murder the people of my village. Our priest, Father Roberto, tried to defend them. They tied him to a post and whipped him till there was nothing left of his robes but bloody rags in the dirt. He was a brave man but no one could help him."

Brantly could not help but feel the pain in Juanito as he told his tale with a contained effort to hide his emotions. Brantly thought that some of Rojas's victims were part of Juanito's family. "You don't look like much of a warrior to me. How can you help us?"

"I know where your horse is kept. There are many guards. The place is very strong. You would need a hundred men to attempt an attack. I am not a warrior, I am a carpenter. But I have the will and the desire. I have taught myself to use this gun. I can shoot well. My father built the hacienda for Rojas. I was a little boy when he took me with him to work every day."

Each of the men listened with rapt attention to the young Mexican. "I know the house, the buildings, better than Rojas. There are secret places. Old tunnels, entrances to mines and underground storage. What looks like shelves of books are doors to secret passages. I can draw these things for you. It is said he has a treasure in gold and silver from years of raiding and robbing."

# 7

A humble abode of stacked stones and plastered adobe baked in the sun on the Mexican side of the Rio Grande. A curtain flapped out a window in a small breeze. Chickens prowled the yard for meager pickens.

Led by an imperious Manuel Rojas on a fine, high-stepping black stallion, a small group of mounted men approached out of the dust. The two Mexicans, Domingo and Alejandro, who stole Zarco, and the Comanche, Mato, were among them. They rode to the door of the hovel. Rojas called, "Hola." When no one responded, he nodded to one of his bandits who dismounted and charged into the house with his gun ready. He came out shaking his head. Rojas spits and turns his black horse away.

A small tributary from the river had formed an idyllic pool fed by water falling. A young woman stood just above waist deep in the water, naked. She held her thick with soap, pitch black hair under the waterfall to rinse it. Rojas and his murderous band of filth arrived next to the rock where she'd left her clothes. Her unadorned beauty was breathtaking. She was caught by surprise at the sound of her name.

"Valentina. Como está?" Rojas looked down from his perch on the black horse. Valentina dropped in the water to her chin wrapping her arms in front of her breasts.

"Where is your Papa?"

"Watering the sheep. He is coming soon to eat."

Domingo stepped down to play with her clothes. "This is a good place to wait for him, no?" He looked to Rojas.

"It's better than watching chickens." Rojas tongue rested on his lower lip as he chuckled. Mato remained silent as he fingered a trio of scalps strung on rawhide hanging from his saddle.

Rojas said, "There will be some men, gringos. They will cross the Rio, looking. I want to know when and how many. When you see them, you will come and tell me."

"Why should we? You steal our money. You take our food. We owe you nothing."

He looked at her without emotion and said, "I let you live. If I don't have word from you in one week, even if you see nothing, I will kill your sheep. That I promise to you." As he turned his horse, he called back over his shoulder, "Tell your Papa." Then as he rode by the others, "Mato, I know you are hungry for a woman. Why not use this one? But I want her alive when you are finished with her. Alejandro, you stink. Take a bath. Domingo, all of you stink like something dead, take a bath." They whooped and hollered as they stepped down and started to pull off their clothes and wade into the water.

Valentina, terrified, looked desperately for somewhere, somehow, a place of escape. She moved under the waterfall as they approached. Her screams and cries where muffled by the sound of falling water. Rojas smiled a gleaming white smile. He thought about his waiting Encarnita and his priceless new stallion as he loped away.

♣

Brantly had told Juanito to gather his gear and meet him at Sir Lionel's ranch. Their wagon was being loaded with an assortment of unusual supplies. Wilford had come back to read it out to be sure. "Six kegs of nails, four wire cutters, three cases of dynamite, half a dozen iron skillets? You plannin' on a lot of cookin'?"

The front door opened by a man standing there. He wore a low-crowned hat, a frock coat and two guns. He spotted Brantly and said, "I don't know why I'm here. I find it difficult to credit that I *am* here." It was Taggert Kilman. "And even more aggravating to comprehend is the fact that you *sent* for me. Last time our paths crossed I remember sayin' that if I ever saw you again, I'd kill you."

"If you're still of that mind, now is your chance."

"I'll hear you out first, I can always kill you later."

The other men stood in awe trying to get a grasp on the moment. Clayton jumped forward. "I don't believe we've met." He extended his hand. Taggert glared at him. Did not accept his hand.

Brantly said, "Taggert Kilman doesn't shake hands with anybody. It's easier to kill somebody you don't know."

"Sometimes."

"Clayton Moore, Taggert Kilman," said Brantly.

Taggert nodded. Clayton said, "Heard the name."

"Taggert is the best pistolero I've ever seen. And it pains me to say it. He's just as good with a long gun." And more pointedly to answer Taggert's curiosity, "and that's why I sent for him."

Sir Lionel had been listening and stepped up to them. "Mr. Stormer, may I have the pleasure?"

"I don't know that I'd go that far. Taggert Kilman, this is Sir Lionel Lawson. He will be the man employing us." As they sized each other up without handshakes, Brantly said, "He's been on one side or the other of every scrape from Tombstone to St. Jo. We go back a ways."

"What's the deal?"

"Two thousand dollars."

"Is this stand up, out in the open shootin' or back alley killin'?"

"Could be both. The wages are the same."

"I'm in."

"Have you got a long rifle?"

"Haven't had much call for one."

Lionel said, "I have a custom-made matched pair of Rigbys. They are excellent weapons. Served me very well in Africa on a Cape buffalo at a fair distance."

Digger Carlson had been present, silently attentive. Brantly drew him into the talk of long guns. "Digger here is more than a fair hand with a rifle. I know from a reliable source that he brought down an antelope buck with one clean shot at an impossible distance. We may have to have a contest to see who is best suited to Lionel's rifles."

Digger had a twinkle in his keen eyes. "I'm good with the one I brought. Taggert can have one of Lionel's. That buck you mentioned was standing still." He smiled.

"I heard a normal man couldn't tell if it was a buck or a bush."

Digger just smiled as he rolled a smoke. Brantly pulled a pocket watch and opened the cover. "I've got one more man to meet us here. Then we can head back to the ranch."

"And who will that be?" Lionel asked.

"Name is Mathew Brawls. He's a fighting man. He needs a battle. I had the opportunity to talk with him once. He was born to it. He is an attacker. Doesn't care what the odds are. Show him the enemy, his only concern is to destroy him. He has destruction in the deepest part of him. He charges forward. He will not stop killing. If an enemy is alive, he's not beaten. I am pleased he's consented to join us. He will be of great value. As I remember, he lacked a close relationship with soap."

The loaded wagon had left for the ranch with Clayton and Digger. Brantly and Lionel stood on the porch at the entrance to the Cougar Gap Trading Post. Far as they could see in any direction the plains were empty, flat, and dry under a blue sky. Brantly checked his watch. A spec moving appeared on the far horizon. They watched it approach through the shimmering waves of heat.

Mathew Brawls was a big man, in every sense. He gave the impression he could walk through a wall without a door. He had a jaw you couldn't break with an ax handle. Even though his horse had the size and stout to pack him, the big part-Belgian heaved a sigh as Mathew stepped down and loosened the cinch. He spat a wad of brown juice into the dust. On his left hip, he wore a Bowie knife. A fourteen-inch blade, two inches wide with a bone handle made it a formidable weapon, a short sword. Mathew spent a fair amount of time in a meditative state honing it to shave his arm.

♣

Trey Gowdy had been in love with Amanda since his first glimpse. He was a good hand and admired her skill with horses. He had no male problems with learning from a woman and was always eager to absorb what he could to improve his own considerable ability. He was the best horseman on the ranch. Sir Lionel kept Amanda informed of their efforts to rescue Zarco. She had been the first to think beyond the limits of the law and come up with the idea of forming their own band of redeemers. She was respectful of the fact that it was man's work and left them to it.

Though unsure of the depth of her feeling for him, she was grateful for Trey's attention, his help, and the diversion of working with the other horses. Trey held a secret that no one knew. There was a convicted criminal in his family, a brother. Peyton

Gowdy had always been a wild seed as if blown into the world on a stormy wind and taken root in ground owned by a family to which he never felt he belonged. He'd been in prison for five years. A man had been killed in a confused, entangled situation. It was never proven who pulled the trigger. Peyton was involved and went to prison as an accomplice.

Brantly had been involved as a Texas Ranger and had known Peyton before the event that put him in prison. He'd witnessed a fair, out on the street, gunfight in which Peyton was outnumbered by a bunch of murdering brothers who had burned a family of settlers they'd robbed and killed. With staggering speed and accuracy, when the smoke cleared, Peyton was the only one standing. Brantly payed for the drinks and never forgot it.

Peyton had been released from prison two days ago. Trey was aware of the fact. He had no idea what to expect. Brantly did. He had hired Peyton to be one of his band of 'liberators'.

Trey was first-born by two years. He was fair in his coloring. He stood in the swirling dust as a colt galloped a circle around Amanda. He swung a rope softly and tossed it out at the colt's feet moving by. Just getting him comfortable with the action. He was coiling the rope to repeat the action when he noticed a rider at the distant gate talking to one of the hands with a rifle who opened the gate. The rider came through and headed toward the pen.

Trey turned to Amanda. "I'll be back." He walked out of the pen to meet the rider.

Out of the sun, in the library lined with books, Brantly was gathered with, Sir Lionel, Taggert Kilman, Mathew Brawls, Digger Carlson, and Juanito Torres. Lionel was still absorbing what Brantly had just told him about hiring Trey's brother Peyton. "I didn't know Trey even had a brother. He's always been a quiet lad." Lionel said.

"I didn't know Peyton had a brother till I told him about you." Brantly walked to the window and moved the drape. "There they are, meetin up right now."

Lionel went to the window shaking his head. "I'll be...this is bound to be interesting. Let's just give them some time together. Five years..." He shook his head again.

That night he spent some quiet time with Amanda. As he listened to her talk and ask questions he was taken away from the moment by seeing his wife in his daughter. The love of his life, Camilla, had left her brand on Amanda. Her constant presence in his life was a living portrait of Camilla. She was never satisfied with her disobedient hair and when tucking in a wayward lock would refer to it as if it were a willful child.

Though Amanda could barely walk when Camilla passed, she had the same habit with her hair. The same love of flowers and trees. He marveled at that and smiled. He had never mentioned it and thought that he should. "So what do you think about Trey's brother?"

"He's a handsome devil. Apart from that, they couldn't be more unalike."

"I agree. He's an absolute stranger."

"Far as I know they've had no physical contact whatsoever. Not even a handshake."

"He has the look of a gunman. There's the aura of threat about him." Lionel had taken in the way he wore his guns. One in a holster and one pearl-handled, tucked into the gun belt for a cross draw. Not your typical cowboy.

"Amanda said, "Mr. Brantly has certainly put together an interesting collection of individuals."

"And they're not all here yet. Mr. Dynamite is yet to arrive. I believe that in Brantly's life he has known someone who is good at anything you can imagine and some who are good at things that would never come to your mind."

"We just have to figure what we need and see if I can come up with an expert with cajones," was the way he had put it.

Lionel had responded with, "What we need are men who can become ten of themselves in an instant."

The early morning misty dust was beginning to dry when Clayton drove a wagon through the gate. He pulled up next to the smaller bunkhouse. Sitting beside him was a tall lean man with a pale shining face and a wonky eye under a rumpled black felt. Brantly came out to greet them. Humphrey "Stick" Comstock climbed down with joints in need of lubrication and shook hands. He did not smile. Then for no reason that anyone could tell, he burst into a boisterous laugh that shook the ground and took some time to abate.

His one eye appeared to be looking off to the left while the other looked straight ahead. It gave him a wild, crazy expression. He gave the impression that he might suddenly howl and spring at someone. And indeed he might.

While he hauled a sizable satchel into the bunkhouse following Clayton, Brantly addressed his curious gang, wanting each to know as much as they could about each other. "He's an artist with explosives. A man he'd worked with said, 'Stick could blow up a saddle and leave the horse wearing it standin' without a hair turned.'"

# 8

There was a bigger establishment for sportin
women in Wolfpaw but it was ten miles beyond
the Cougar Gap Trading Post and its paltry pair of
prostitutes. It boasted a larger clientele, trail
herding cowboys, Mexican bandits with no care
for borders, Comanche half-breeds, and any other
travelers who were just passing through. Peyton
Gowdy found it even before he found Quail Run
Ranch and his brother, Trey.

Peyton had a sense of his life dripping
through his fingers faster than he could take a holt.
He never possessed whatever it was that caused
young men to pine about young women. Brass-
nutted from birth, he was naturally more inclined
toward combat. When biological urges occurred he
was content with self-satisfaction and whores.
After five years in prison, female flesh took on an
unaccustomed charm. At least for the moment.

Boss Brantly presided over a meeting with his
desperadoes. It concluded with the conviction that
Manuel Rojas was profoundly protected and to
find a way to penetrate his security would be a
challenge, indeed. The sun had set leaving a purple
dusk running to black. Peyton muttered to himself
as he put a foot in a stirrup and rode through the
gate toward the faint trail to Wolfpaw.

The cowboy had a thin pattern of pale hairs decorating his unshaven face and an assortment of pimples. He had waited longer than he felt was tolerable for his turn with the jug-breasted redhead Peyton had paid for and was enjoying. The cowboy had used his time to stare at the door and consume far more Tequila than prudent. As Peyton came out of the room at an unhurried pace, the cowboy grabbed him by his waistcoat and jerked him aside. Peyton instantly gathered himself with the quickness of a leopard and brisked up knowing that he must not intensify the situation to avoid any chance of returning to prison. The cowboy was unwilling to quit and moved with speed toward Peyton who stepped aside and pushed pimple-puss into the wall with a thud. He bounced back with his gun drawn, his face squinched like a closing accordion. Peyton kicked him in his nuts. He dropped his gun as he curled and tumbled down the long flight of stairs. He landed in a heap unmoving on the floor below. Jug-breasts had watched it all from her parted door. Peyton flew down the stairs, leapt over pimples, and darted out to the street where his horse waited. He departed with alacrity.

There was snoring that rattled window panes and mumbles of a card game when Peyton climbed into his bunk next to Stick Comstock, still awake and staring. Peyton couldn't tell where the stare was directed. "I've never been able to feel comfortable about the idea of being with a whore. So, I've never tried it. Tell me about how you feel about that."

Peyton took a minute to absorb what he'd heard. He adjusted his pillow to raise his head. "It's not complicated. I've never thought about it. For me it's as simple as chowin down when you're hungry. When your belly's full you just push back and leave the table."

Stick turned to lean on his elbow and look at Peyton. "Don't you never feel anything about the woman?"

"No sir. Never give it a thought. I have never cared to wake in the morning to the scent of a woman from the night before. I prefer the aroma of cows and horses, mesquite and dew. If I could get that into a bottle, I could sell a boxcar full up in New York city. Those dandies need help to smell like a man instead of a daisy." He smiled and shook his head. "Whores keep it simple."

Stick rolled on to his back to stare at the ceiling and look into his mind. His voice was soft and distant like the rustle of dried leaves in a breeze. "When my wife died, I thought my life was over. I just wanted to curl up and quit. I'd lahk to find another woman lahk her but hell, I live in the middle of nowhere with a herd of goats. Not much chance of meetin a woman lahk her out there. Sides, my looks tend to put folks off."

♣

Two ranch hands, Buck Taylor and String Bean sat with kegs of nails between them. With heavy wire cutters they cut nails in half and loaded them into the kegs. The sun was just up and beginning to bake the morning when the sharp sound of a rifle shot shattered the stillness.

Taggert Kilman sat with knees up, elbows pressed against them to hold the rifle rock steady. At almost 200 yards away three playing cards were tacked to a tree. The ace of spades had just been struck, dead center. Taggert ejected the shell and loaded another. He pressed his cheek to the stock, lined his eye to the scope, drew a breath, let half out and held the rest as he squeezed the trigger. The ace of hearts was struck, dead on. The same thing occurred with the ace of diamonds.

Brantly, Lionel, Mathew Brawls, Peyton, Stick Comstock, Juanito, Digger Carlson and Clayton had all been watching, duly impressed. At a slightly shorter distance, Digger Carlson used his own rifle with iron sights and both eyes open. Three new cards were drilled with like accuracy and astonishing speed. Everyone's spirits were soaring with confidence in their brothers in arms. Brantly breathed with satisfaction and turned to Lionel. "Lionel, your turn."

He began to protest in a modest manner but was immediately cut short by Brantly and Taggert, who said, "Come on, Sir, we wanna see if you just own em, or can you shoot em?"

Lionel smiled and walked over to the log where the rifles and ammo were laid out. He reached into the red velvet-lined leather case and took out the gleaming mate to the one that Taggert had used. Lionel was a tall, lean, athletic man who moved with an easy, graceful elegance. He presented an atmosphere of quiet power with no effort. He took a position at the line of fire. There weren't any more aces. Juanito asked if he had a preference. "I like the number three. Let us have threes."

With a minimum of precise, effortless movement and never lifting his cheek from the stock, he drilled all of the number three cards in rapid succession. Then he looked up to the stunned group as Taggert led the applause. "I think we give you a new name, Sir Sniper."

Juanito held their attention out of the blistering heat in the smaller bunkhouse. He had prepared drawings of Rojas's stronghold in detail. With a sketch of the surrounding area he explained the existence of a hidden tunnel constructed by

Spaniards many years before the building of Rojas' hacienda, it was for the purpose of escape from invaders. It remained long unused.

♣

Brantly decided to take Taggert and Peyton with him on a scouting expedition. The sun had begun its plunge toward the western horizon as a quarter moon floated in. They paused at the Rio Grande and looked across. Brantly urged his sorrel mare into the water. Taggert and Peyton followed. They emerged in Mexico and headed upriver. The humble home of Jesus Galindo and his beautiful daughter, Valentina stood silently unlit in the approaching darkness. Brantly asked his mare to halt and called to the house, "Señor Galindo? Señorita…Valentina. Hola, it's Brantly Stormer." He listened and heard a voice from within.

The old man cracked the door and said, "Brantly?"

"Yes. It's me. Brantly."

Jesus was old and bent. He shuffled through the door. "Oh, Señor Brantly," he lifted the lamp he carried. "It has been too much years." Brantly stepped down and moved to the old man to embrace him.

"You have been gone too long, Brantly Stormer. Our house has been empty without your friendship."

"I have missed you, Jesus. Where is Valentina?"

"In the house. You will come in."

Brantly moved to his horse and took a package from his saddle bag. He handed it to Jesus. "There is some tobacco, you like. And something for Valentina."

"Come, come to the house."

They entered the hovel. It was neat and clean. Two chairs, a table, a stool on the dirt floor. A curtain separated the main room from space behind. Valentina was at the stone fireplace. Brantly knew something was not right when she did not turn to greet him. "Valentina, did you not hear me? It's Brantly."

"Yes, Papa, I know." She still had not turned to face him. She brought cups to the table but averted her head so as not to be seen. "Sit down, Brantly. It is so good to see you." She could not continue to avoid being seen and turned to face him.

Brantly was stunned by the severity of her swollen bruises. They were purple, red, yellow swellings. They screamed of pain. One eye was totally closed. Brantly could not contain the rapid rising of seething wrath. He rose slowly and took her gently in his arms.

Jesus said, "It was a warning. If we do not tell him when the men come looking for the horse, it will be worse."

Brantly stroked her hair with the softness of a feather. "You will tell him."

Valentina pulled away. "No! No!"

Brantly took her back into his arms and brought her head to his shoulder. "You will tell him. Tell him that men have come looking. You do not know who the men are. They would say nothing."

♣

Mato, the scalp collecting Comanchero, was an incarnation of evil. He was all bad. He took pure pleasure from inflicting pain and death upon living creatures. Cries, shrieks, and howls of victims were music to his frenzied brain. Manuel Rojas valued Mato as a fearless warrior. He came and went as he pleased. Usually alone. He mounted his horse and rode across the lot in front of the barn toward the guarded gate. It swung open for him. He knuckled the sealed socket minus an eye, smoothed his twenty-past-eight mustache and rode into the twilight, in the direction of Cougar Gap.

Both Peyton and Taggert immediately sensed a man transformed from the one who entered the house of Jesus only minutes before. Brantly normally moved in a nimble fluid manner. He seemed to have turned to stone as he mounted his mare without a word and turned her away from the house. They followed.

His contained fury was palpable as they closed in on each side and rode in silence. His face seemed as if he were to speak, it would crack and crumble like avalanching rock. "They raped his daughter." A hardness had formed in his chest, a stone of hatred. It gave his voice the sound of a man trying to speak while being hung. Brantly had long found Valentina to be a woman of singular beauty. In every sense. It had been a passing thing that only stayed for a while till some other concern took its place. But before long the image of Valentina would come to his mind and for a time bring him pleasure. The thought of her being savaged by such filth as Rojas' men was more than he could bear.

Rojas' long-standing dominance over the area he ruled with terror at the sound of his name, was bred from fear. They were gentle, timid, hard-scrabble peasants with no leadership, no weapons. His success at control, robbing and stealing had fostered a sense of security. He had come to think of himself as omnipotent. Like his Comanche savage, Mato, he had no conscience, no sense of morality. He cared only for his wealth and power. In the narrow corridors of his arrogance he'd come to believe he was untouchable.

To the extent that his adversaries were dim-witted in their faulty confidence, Juanito Torres was wise beyond his experience. Brantly was quick to see it and realize that Juanito was an asset of far greater value than what he'd thought.

Juanito had been to the cock-fights at the big six-sided structure a mile from Cougar Gap in an isolated grove. His cousin, Raul, had a small operation going with one breeding rooster and had produced a few good killer birds. Juanito acted as a 'second' when he had the time. He'd seen some of Rojas' men there as spectator gamblers. A few were there seeking fame and fortune with their own home-bred birds.

Tenacious images of Valentina being violated by Mato ran through Brantly's mind without pause. The force of venomous hatred consumed his being. Juanito told him that no one at the cockfights had any knowledge of himself. "I am just another Mexican. But I have knowledge of them. I have seen Mato. Many times, alone. He does not know me. Even the one who cut my neck. He ran thinking I was dead."

They rode out at dusk into the still, purple glow. Brantly, Juanito, Taggert and Peyton, four cowboys with a night away from their herd. Brantly had been without sleep since he rode away from Jesus's house the night before. He'd been silent, except for brief exchanges with Juanito.

It was dark when they topped a low rise on the flat prairie and saw the 'arena' a half-mile away. With help from a dim moon and lanterns, one could see a crowd gathering to gain entrance. The sound of voices and guitars drifted to the riders. Peyton said, "This thing's got some popularity to it. That's a congregation down there."

Brantly eased his mare forward. He looked to Juanito. "Might be better if you go in on your own. Try to not look like we're all together." Juanito trotted forward.

A fat gringo sat in a chair by the door and took a dollar from each person wanting inside. The chatter came together as a foreign sound. The corrugated roof sent its own gathered heat down into the smoke-filled cylinder emitting a blend of sweat, garlic and onions, beer and whiskey. The seats were tiered benches being filled with cowboys, big men in overalls, Mexicans and waspy Asians. The smell of smoke, feathers, hot bird shit and sweating unwashed people could be sliced.

Below was a rectangular pit with two fenced areas at each end. A skinny Asian, the color of beeswax, entered with a sack of flour and poured lines in the dirt. A referee and two handlers holding beautiful birds with knives attached to one leg entered. One handler was Mexican, paunchy and soft. His bird was brilliantly multicolored and glossy red-headed. The other was iridescent green, held by a leathery old man. The men shook hands with a hint of a nod and holding the birds to face each other, blew a blast of breath right at their rectums ruffling their feathers apart. They allowed the birds to peck at each other to get them fired up. The men separated, stepped behind the flour lines and released their birds. They rushed at each other with a singular purpose.

The redhead leaped on the green, stabbing. The green struck hard with a wing causing a dull pop from red's leg. Red slashed with his good leg and caused a spout of blood to spurt from green's beak and he fell to the ground. The handlers rushed in, picked up their birds and blew into their mouths. They set them back on the line. The redhead charged and tried for a slashing blow with his good leg as the green thrashed him with a powerful thrust from his wing. Blood dripped from its beak and it fell dead. The old man picked up his bird by one leg and tossed it toward the shadows in the back.

The bond between these men and their birds was unique. There was no affection or fondness. There was however a matter of pride, a mingling of psyches with their sleek beauty and compelling danger. Their careers were often brief, ending in death.

There was constant movement in the audience between contests. People changing seats, leaving and returning. Brantly knew Juanito was there somewhere but had not seen him until he felt his presence behind him as he stooped close to his ear. "He is here. I will walk behind him and signal with my head." He moved on to blend with the crowd. Peyton sat to Brantly's left and heard. Taggert had not heard the words but was aware of the exchange. Brantly's eyes followed Juanito around to the other side of the arena. He moved easily in an unhurried, aimless manner. He barely paused behind Mato sitting with two other men. He glanced across to Brantly, jutted his chin at the top of Mato's head, then shuffled off.

Brantly felt an immediate tightening of the knotted rope in his chest. Peyton and Taggert saw it all. A quick glance passed among them. Brantly drew a breath and turned his head as if to look in another direction but his eyes remained focused on the Comanchero smoking a cigarillo. Mato looked straight down at the preparations for the next fight, paying no mind to the hombre filling his ear. Brantly thought about getting up, taking the path Juanito had, walking up behind the greasy killer and putting two bullets into the back of his head and seeing his face blow off against the man in front.

He stepped outside and drew the night air deep into his chest. Taggert and Peyton stood in the shadows, mounted, holding Brantly's mare, *Tree Fightin Woman.* He took the reins and put his foot in the stirrup.

In the pale blue muted light one could just make out the trail they sought. A small disturbance in the scrubby mesquite became Juanito riding softly to join them. "He will come this way. He is alone," he whispered. They moved into some low trees and vanished. "How do you want to do this?" Taggert whispered.

"I want to kill him." Brantly just mouthed the words.

"How?"

"Watch."

They didn't wait long before hearing the horse walking toward them. They all tensed watching Brantly for some sign. He had lifted his reins just an inch and the mare came up on her toes. He raised his hand signaling the others to stay behind. He spurred her bursting out of the trees at a full run. Mato tried to turn to avoid the charging mare as she slammed into his horse with the force of a train. Brantly kept his seat and the mare kept her feet. Mato's horse went down throwing him hard. He struggled to his feet reaching for his gun. Brantly dismounted and charged right into him knocking him back to the ground. When he turned his head he saw a boot coming right at his eye. Brantly had kicked him so hard in the face it seemed his head would roll. He spat out blood and teeth. He got to his feet as Brantly knocked him down again and mashed his face into the dirt with his boot. Peyton and Taggert had arrived, while Juanito stayed in the shadows. Peyton said, "I don't believe I've seen anybody that pissed off. He's gonna kill him."

"He said he wanted to," Taggert offered.

"Looks like he will," said Peyton.

Brantly kicked Mato's gun away as he grabbed a handful of hair and dragged him to a rock and slung his head into it again and again. Brantly was black with rage. Peyton and Taggert were stunned by what they were witnessing. "I believe he's done killed him." Peyton looked at Taggert. Brantly slammed Mato's head into the rock once more and dropped him. He turned a black look to them. He was beyond reason. Peyton stepped down and walked over to take a look. "This is one Comanche that don't look too troublesome."

Brantly seemed to have begun to come a little out of his rage. "He raped and killed young girls and old women. He scalped their men. He made them watch." His voice was glacial.

Juanito stared, listening. He showed no expression. Taggert said, "Is he dead?"

Peyton looked closer. "Can't tell."

"He will be when I cut his throat," Brantly said. It was a rasping sound, words struggling to get out.

"You may not have to."

"I'll do it anyway. That's how I want him found."

Clayton was still in the house telling Lionel what had occurred. No one gathered in the bunkhouse with their coffee had been to sleep when the cock crowed. Peyton stood possessed, addressing the men with gruesome details of the dark events of the night. Each man was silent, absorbing the facts as Peyton laid them out. He was still in awe of the power of Brantly's rage. "I believe he was too hot to touch. Never seen that." Leaving them with the image of Mato's head nearly severed from his body, he ceased speaking and blew out a breath.

Juanito had listened in silence, reliving his nightmares with every word. Perhaps out of some need to defend Brantly's action, he stepped forward with his head down and in almost a whisper, said, "I was there to see what Mato and his savages did. I was hiding, watching, afraid to breathe." He had scrambled into a cramped cabinet and pulled the door shut. It would not stay closed. The sounds of violence forced it to ease open an inch. He could hear his family screaming, pottery crashing, furniture being tossed. "Señor Brantly's anger was the anger I have carried for years. His hands did the dreams that have kept me from sleep. I could feel what he felt but I could not do what he did." He took a deep breath and blew it out. "Now my pain is not so heavy." No one spoke.

# 9

Unless he'd drunk himself to sleep, Manuel Rojas was usually up to see the sun rise. His live-in whore, Encarnita, remained abed while he took his coffee down to the courtyard and then to the stable to check on his special horses. Zarco was kept in a large stall with an outdoor pen attached. He stopped there first. The stallion came to the door and stretched his neck to Rojas who gently raised his hand to circle his fingers lightly between the warm brown eyes. Sergio was issuing orders to his stable hands. Vaqueros had begun to tend to ranch chores while sleepy guards left their posts to the day shift. They had grown used to the fear that Hacienda del Diablo had represented and the lasting lack of threat that resulted. They were not the most vigilant sentinels.

Rojas stood by the half-door of a stall at the far end. The sensitive feminine head of a young mare reached over to accept his soft stroking of her face. He fondled her velvet nostrils running his thumb and forefinger around the edge and pulling gently, which she seemed to enjoy. She took a deep breath and blew a mist of snot. He laughed, "Soon you will be a mamacita." He strolled away. One of his Comanchero night guards approached in an unconcerned manner to inform the *"General"* that Mato had not yet returned to the hacienda.

"He probably fell asleep inside some fat whore." Rojas laughed. "Tell the guard to let me know when he returns."

♣

A sense of decorum came with Lionel's heritage. He used all at his disposal to inform Amanda of the most recent event without distressing details. He sat listening to Brantly in the saddle/bunkhouse. All his men were present.

"Rojas's world will change when they find Mato. He knows that stealing the horse will not go unanswered. Juanito and I will make a plan."

♣

Comanches and Mexicans had a long, violent, complex and ever changing relationship. At times they were sworn enemies, at others, they formed alliances based on current needs and desires. Never predictable, always, uncertain, loyalty was never an issue. They often bred and produced Comancheros. A young bandit came at a full gallop toward the gate to Hacienda del Diablo. The gate opened. He charged through and rode up to the courtyard calling to the guard. Rojas came out to hear that Mato had been found. A wagon and three men were sent.

Rojas looked down at the encrusted, battered remains covered with flies and brought a kerchief to his nose. "He smells the same in death as he did in life. He looks no different. Bashed in face. A few more flies. Build a fire, and send him up in smoke." He waved the kerchief in dismissal to the men at the wagon.

Her lounging gown flowing loosely, Encarnita flung herself on the bed. "So who do you think did him?"

"It would be difficult to make a list of those who would *not* like to see him like this."

"What about the people you took the horse from?"

"It is possible." He paused to consider. "But I think it is too violent for them." He poured bMathew into a glass. She patted the bed next to her.

# 10

Juanito moved his pencil with authority and skill over the papers spread on the table. "I have been there a few times and gone inside. It is very dark and winding through the rock. I can find it. But we must be very careful to not be seen."

"You say it was built by the Spaniards?" Brantly examined the sketches.

"As an escape tunnel, many, many years ago."

"Where does it go?"

"I do not know. I've never gone to the end. It was too far. I was alone in the dark and frightened."

"We will go together. You and me." Brantly smiled at Juanito, just a crease at one corner of his mouth. The young man smiled and picked up his pencil to resume drawing.

It was velvet, blue-black; the sliver of moon behind a slow-moving rumpled cloud. All was dead silent. Their horses were secured below in a dense copse to the side of a narrow cut through rock. They moved without sound uphill through brush to a pile of rocks. Juanito lifted a heavy rock and handed it to Brantly who placed it aside. They continued until an opening began to show itself.

Juanito crawled into the black hole and reached back for Brantly to hand him a torch ready to be lit once well into the darkness. The light would not be seen from outside. Brantly crawled in and struck a match. The torch revealed a space filled with webs. Juanito could almost stand up to his full height. Brantly had to bend but not crawl. They moved with caution, lighting the way ahead to see where to place their feet. The tunnel twisted and turned to follow the way of least resistance to the diggers.

Nearly half an hour brought them to a solid plank wall ending the tunnel and concealing what lay beyond. It seemed immoveable, tight at the sides and bottom. It showed no signs of use. Brantly probed with his fingers around the edges and along the top. He discovered two stout hinges. He pulled his knife from its sheath and dug along the bottom scraping dirt away. It seemed that one board might slide from a notch in the side wall. There was nothing to grip to make it move. He moved the torch to search the area. He found a hefty rock to use as a hammer and handed the torch to Juanito. He pounded his knife solidly into the plank as a handle and managed to work the board loose.

In the end they were able to lift the plank wall up on its hinges and prop it open. A small space showed a wood floor with a trap door. They lifted the door and looked down into a grain storage bin, well-built and home to a bevy of barn rats at a banquet. They quickly shut the door and backed away. They were right above the stable at Hacienda del Diablo. They put everything back as they found it and made their way back down to their horses. Leaving no sign of having been there, they dissolved into the night.

The sun was an hour from rising as Brantly and Juanito sat in the bunkhouse with fresh coffee. A few sheets of paper on the table in front of them were filled with sketches as Juanito continued to draw floor plans of the stable and courtyard from memory.

Taggert Kilman and Digger Carlson joined them with plates of eggs and bacon and biscuits. Sir Lionel saw to it that his men were well-kept. He believed in the importance of a good breakfast.

Brantly had assigned the two sharpshooters along with Peyton who had the watchful gaze of a raptor, a delicate task. They were to explore the country around them to discover different approaches to Rojas' stronghold. They were to make no effort to not be seen but rather to appear as cowboys on a casual quest for drifting cattle. They'd started early in the morning, the day before, while Brantly and Juanito planned their stealthy search in the dark for the tunnel.

"How'd it go?" Brantly looked to both men.

Taggert spoke. "Good. We got separated from Peyton for a while. Two villains rode up and wanted to know what we were up to. Only one spoke, he was a 'beaner', he said it would be wise for us to go no further. The other was a Comanchero. He just looked surly and dirty, said nothing, glared."

"Digger?" Brantly shifted his gaze.

Digger's bright eyes shined as he wiggled his mustache. "We found several good places where a man could hide and shoot. We couldn't see the hacienda from where we were but we could tell it could be seen from these places. One would have to climb on foot. But it looks good and possible. I'd say we set-up in the dark have someone take the horses and be ready to bring them back for a quick getaway. Keep the site clean and unknown. Use it again."

♣

Mathew Brawls, using a stout wire cutter, had spent most of the day cutting nails in half from a wooden keg. They would be used as part of the dynamite to a devastating effect. He was out of tobacco and missed the customary lump in his face. He saddled his big horse and rode off in the muted twilight still pink before dark. Cougar Gap

Trading Post was a welcome sight, a faint glowing in the distance.

Having secured his supply of plug tobacco and a small bag of hard candy, he made his way to the large room and the bar at the far end. Though not usually a drinking man, after a long day of cutting nails and the dusty ride, the thought of a little neck-oil became pleasant. The bar was occupied by several men, mostly strangers to each other and a few companions and two whores seeking employment.

Mathew eased up and stood politely back waiting for a little room for his sizable self. Two men separated enough to create a small space. Mathew acknowledged their effort and squeezed in. He gave off an aroma that was strong enough to flatten a bull. He ordered a whiskey. As he raised the glass to his lips, he heard the jingle of spurs behind him as an elbow shoved him aside causing the whiskey to spill over his shirt. He turned to the arrogant surly face of a Comanchero glaring, forcing his way closer to the bar. Mathew stood fast and roughly blocked any advancement knocking the Comanchero off balance. He was one of the two who had confronted Taggert and Digger. He was also part of the gang who had raped Valentina when she bathed. He snarled and drew his gun. With blurring speed, Mathew grabbed the barrel and twisted hard. A loud pop was heard from the snapping of the Comanchero's trigger finger. He howled in pain. Mathew jerked the uncocked gun free of his grip and in one fluid movement, snatched the Comanchero's hat from his head with his left hand, while his right swung an arc that ended with the butt of the gun crunching the man's skull above his left ear. The bandana that tightly wrapped his head contained the fragments of bone as blood poured through. He dropped like a sack of grain. The room was awe struck, dead silent. Mathew looked down at the heap of filth on the floor, turned and left. No one moved.

On the ride back, Mathew wished he'd had the opportunity to finish his whiskey in peace. All of Brantly's men knew the value of an eye for detail. Even Stick with his wonky eye was not deprived of accurate observation. When Mathew described the event at Cougar's Gap, both Taggert and Digger agreed it was the same son-of-a-bitch with the Mexican who warned them to go no further. Rojas and his men had been accustomed to living with impunity. It was a lawless time in a lawless land. Trying to determine who was responsible for anything criminal was never even considered. Hangings were common, clumsy and hasty, with no one of authority in attendance other than the ones who tightened the nooses and sent the horses out from under. Witnesses never came forward.

Brantly had listened carefully. "Was he dead?"

"I expect so. He was sure bent on killin me."

"Rojas will send men sneaking around to see what they can. We need to be diligent in protecting this place. We must make it clear to anyone who comes close that they will be killed."

Peyton said, "How do we do that?"

"By killing the first ones that come," Brantly said in a hoarse whisper.

"That'll be war."

"That's what this is. All Rojas has is an overblown reputation for scaring people. His men are lazy drunks who can't shoot, have no training, and no real reason to fight. They get what they want just by being part of his gang. No one ever challenges them."

Brantly with Taggert and Peyton patrolled every inch of the area around Quail Run Ranch and all of the possible approaches. They set up a system of round-the-clock guards posted near every path of access to Lionel's ranch. Amanda was not to leave the ranch under any circumstances.

*Alex Cord*

# 11

The Comanches as a unified fighting force had been largely defeated. They existed in small scattered groups of elders, women and children out on the plains. The younger ones had become renegades, breeding with Mexicans, surviving by robbing, raping and killing defenseless settlers coming west. These made up the bulk of Rojas's gang of cutthroats. Comancheros were undisciplined, unpaid, savages who knew nothing of loyalty. Human life had no value other than as an object for abuse and torture. Even their own life and death held little concern for the Comanchero, making them the most frightening of foes. Rojas held sway by his swift willingness to kill an insurgent instantly.

Under cover of a black night with Juanito as guide Brantly took Stick Comstock and sharp-eyed Peyton to the narrow pass near the entrance to the tunnel. They moved without sound or light until inside the tunnel. Peyton stood guard while Stick planned the use of his dynamite both inside the tunnel and in the narrow gap, which was the main passageway in and out of the hacienda. Between its vertical walls it was wide enough to allow a wagon to pass through.

The bandits of Manuel Rojas were a disorganized bunch of opportunists, pistoleros, who sought the flimsy security of a place to sleep with guarded walls in exchange for their contributions to Rojas's treasure chest. Nothing bound them beyond their desire to be there and the animal instinct that hunters have greater success in a pack than alone. There was some advantage in the menacing reputation of Hacienda del Diablo. Apart from them and the Comancheros were the Vaqueros, skilled horsemen and good hands with cattle. Their boss was Sergio who maintained a vegetable garden and a wife while managing the care and breeding of the horses. The cattle were vast herds of mixed breeds mostly stolen. Rojas had no real interest in the cattle other than to annoy the Texans by stealing them. It was not uncommon for bold Texans to cross the river and raid the Mexican herds to run off with hundreds of cattle that were actually theirs to begin with. The raids were often accomplished without shots being fired.

♣

Though he liked to think of himself as a general and to be addressed as such, he was in reality far from a military man. He lacked the discipline, the training, and the mind for organization and planning. He was as wily as a wolf but as dumb as a box of rocks. He could not bring together a group of men to discuss a problem and a plan for solving it.

Who would he ask the question, "Who do you think killed Mato?" and expect a useful answer? The true answer would be, *anyone*. The same would be true of the Comanchero Mathew Brawls left in a heap on the floor of Cougar Gap Trading Post. Were these normal hazards of the lives they led or were they part of something more sinister? These were the questions running through his mind. He had no one to share them with. Thoughts of the Englishman began to run in his mind. There had been no response from him since Rojas took his horse. He could not put it together, the death of two of his most violent men with no traceable clues to anyone, certainly not the Englishman.

The old Mexican, Jesus, father of Valentina, had reported to Rojas that men had come to ask questions but had not returned. Rojas decided to send two men to Sir Lionel's ranch; to get as close as possible without being detected, to learn whatever they could and report back.

They were Comanche half-breeds. Their ability to move without sound was in their blood. Peyton's ability to see movement in the dark was in *his* blood. The Comanche crawled on his belly fifty yards below him. Peyton had his instructions.

He drew a bead and squeezed the trigger. The bullet went right through the top of the Comanche's skull, scattering brains, bone, and blood. He remained where he was. A scurry in the brush revealed just enough of the second man for Peyton to fire again. He had but a fraction of a second and a sliver of target. He imagined where the man's heart would be. He heard the bullet strike with a dull thud. The man did not move.

When their horses returned to Hacienda del Diablo, Manuel Rojas exploded, blindly seeking a target for his rage. He had to determine if his men were victims of protective measures taken by the Englishman to guard his violated property or was it something more ominous? How should he respond? They were in fact intruders on private property. He poured a glass full of brandy while cursing his problems. Encarnita laughed at him and said, "You could just give the horse back to the English. It *is* just a horse." He whirled and slapped her as hard as he could and threw her down on the bed. She flew back at him with bared claws reaching for his eyes. His forearm blocked her attack. He punched her in the face and knocked her to the floor, unconscious.

♣

Stick Comstock had enlisted the aid of Mathew Brawls, Taggert, Juanito, and Digger in the ingenious construction of several bombs made up of dynamite, iron skillets, nails and horseshoes. They varied in size and shape. Stick did not come by his reputation without merit. Brantly was well impressed by the stack of destructive devices. He looked to his gang, each one, with a silent, almost imperceptible nod, a small crease in the corner of his mouth. "When I started this thing, I thought we were just going to steal a horse. I told Juanito we were not going to help him seek revenge. That has all changed. We will destroy this evil plague and leave nothing but ashes. They will not rise again."

They planted their bombs inside the tunnel. With great pains, careful planning and working without sound and remaining unseen, they hid their bombs in crevices, notches and small openings in the vertical walls of the narrow passage in and out of Hacienda del Diablo. It was decided that Peyton's brother, Trey Gowdy, being the best horseman on the ranch, should be the one to ride the stallion Zarco out of the strong hold. He, being in love with Amanda, could not have been more willing. At last he was to be a major part of the rescue plan. He had also taken to sleeping outside the window to her room as an added measure of security.

The failure of the two men Rojas had sent to spy on the Englishman spread throughout the Hacienda the instant their horses showed at the gate. It was a fact of no consequence to one young Comanchero. He was so arrogant in his confidence that he possessed skills far in excess of those of the two dead men, that he allowed a thought to form in his small brain. It would be a huge feather in his cap if he could manage to capture the daughter of the Englishman. He had been raised in a small band of Comanches who taught him the ways of the Comanche warrior. He was skilled in tracking, in using the bow and arrows, in moving without sound, in becoming invisible. There were few who valued these arts anymore and took pride in their worth. He did not have the reasoning power to think beyond the immediate task at hand.

He left his pony way beyond the boundaries of the ranch and made his way on silent moccasins through the tangles of mesquite and chaparral in a soft black night. He'd given no thought to how he would proceed. If he somehow were successful in capturing Amanda, then what? How would he keep her silent? How would he get her away from the ranch? He had not even brought another horse. He thought to have her bound and gagged riding double. It was a suicidal attempt doomed to fail. Had he told anyone at del Diablo they would have told him he was insane. Had he tried to tell General Rojas, he might have been shot.

He succeeded in getting close enough to see the soft flow of her curtains undulating out the open window in the warm breath of the night. His moccasin touched a thin twine that triggered the whoosh of a closing snare. Trey swooped out of the blackness, landing on his back like a cougar on a calf and cut his throat all in one fell swoop, without sound.

Trey had never killed anyone. The thought of protecting the woman he loved eased the way for him to accept what he'd done. He stood looking down, then around to be sure the threat was over. He was surprised to realize that he was calm as he drew a deep breath. The snare and the act of camping near her window was something he'd come up with on his own. Brantly had approved and said nothing about thinking it an unnecessary precaution.

Trey dragged the body off into the brush and went immediately to inform Brantly. He pulled his bandana from his neck and wiped the sweat that now covered his face. In a tremulous voice, short on air, he confessed, "I've never killed anyone before."

Brantly placed his hand lightly on Trey's shoulder for just an instant. "These fiends are the Devil's own disciples." Brantly was vexed to realize that the Comanchero was able to get so close, undetected. An unacceptable vulnerability. "It has fallen on us to rid this world of their presence. I believe it would be reasonable to think of ourselves as soldiers of Christ. Well done, young man."

♣

Sir Lionel Lawson and Clayton had come to the awareness that they were all involved in a much greater endeavor than originally thought. The bodies were beginning to 'pile up'. Even Amanda had made the comment at dinner. "I remember, Daddy, when you first brought up the idea of moving to Texas, I said something about the 'Wild West'. Well here we are." And that was said without knowledge of what had occurred outside her bedroom window. Lionel and Clayton had done their best to keep Amanda as minimally informed of details as possible.

Brantly saddled his mare, *Tree Fightin Woman*, and rode over to visit with Jesus and Valentina. They were never out of his mind. The image of her profound beauty, bruised, battered and swollen was a constant in his life.

He arrived to find that the old man had been beaten when he last reported to Rojas. He hobbled painfully even with the aid of a stick. Valentina had begun to heal. The massive swelling, though still purple and yellow, had subsided to the point that her black-olive eye had begun to open. Brantly felt a carnal stirring in his chest and realized his breath had caught.

Jesus was able to describe in great detail the courtyard and the entrance to Rojas's living quarters and the balcony that looked down on the courtyard.

Brantly knew that the time would come when Valentina and her father would have to leave their home, while the conflict unfolded. He thought to bring them to Lionel's ranch to keep them safe. He made clear how important it was that they do nothing that could provoke Manuel Rojas. "I will return soon." He stood next to his mare with a hand on the old man's shoulder and a warm smile looking down at the sad, helpless, worn face. He turned his gaze to Valentina who smiled valiantly under the glorious veil of brilliant black hair. The urge to reach out and touch her lips with his fingertips rose with a palpable force. Instead he gently took her hand in both of his and brought it to his chest, for a brief time; then put his foot in the stirrup and eased up into the saddle.

All the way back he remained alert to everything around him, while his mind surged with rampant thoughts like a flock of wild birds scattered by a blast. He met with his men over supper. Then he left and moved off to be alone. He built a small fire to serve as a point of focus as one might use a candle. He made a conscious effort to empty his brain. To eliminate thought. To allow other powers the opportunity to function. To concentrate on the simple act of breathing, on the movement of air into his lungs and releasing it out of his lungs.

# 12

The fire had dwindled to a gray bed of smoldering ashes. He tugged at his pocket watch and saw that he'd been there for hours. He pushed away from the tree at his back and stood. He kicked dirt over the ashes and moved off to his bed. After a few hours of sleep, his feet hit the floor as a man refreshed. A man with a plan.

He gathered his troops in the tack room, all of them, including Sir Lionel, Clayton, Trey, and brother Peyton, Juanito, Digger, Stick, Taggert and Mathew Brawls. "Gentlemen, we are going to do something extremely bold and amazing. Therein will lie our success. We are going to exterminate a nest of vipers. They have never been challenged. They are not prepared. They will be shocked by the force of our attack. We will overwhelm them and destroy them. They will think we are a hundred men. They are murderers, thieves, scalpers of men, rapists, killers of women and children. I want you to believe deep in your hearts that we are soldiers of Christ. That we have God on our side." He looked carefully at each individual and saw that he had their eager attention. When his gaze fell on Sir Lionel, he stood and took a step forward.

"This began as repossessing a stolen horse. Not that big a deal in this country. However, it has evolved into something much more important. We are going to free a community of poor, defenseless people, terrorized for years, living in fear of a tyrannical lunatic and his homicidal pack of savages. I'd no idea it would come to this. But it has, and I'm happy to find myself part of this honorable task. I want you all to know that I am completely in accord with Brantly. I have every confidence in each of you, that we will change the lives of countless families once this evil is eliminated. Our reward will be far greater than the satisfaction of getting our horse back." He smiled and moved among the men. "Are there any questions—any doubts? Of course there aren't. I can see that. 'We few, we happy few, we band of brothers.' Shakespeare!" Some scratched their heads and looked askance.

The walls of Lionel's study were covered with books of various descriptions. Brantly held an open copy of Shakespeare's Henry V. "I thought I could read…but this…it's another language…"

Lionel was topping off their whiskeys. "You are not alone, my friend. Many of the world's most educated are thwarted by the genius of Shakespeare. He requires study, but the rewards are enormous. Henry the fifth is a great story of a few men and their belief in a just cause. They are vastly outnumbered by their enemy. Their belief is what wins the day. It's a great story. When you were speaking to the men about the evil we face, it made me think of Henry."

Brantly replaced the book and sat in the big leather chair across the low table from Lionel. He picked up his glass of whiskey and raised it toward Lionel. "To we few, we band of brothers."

"Amen, brother." It was past midnight. The others were all abed except for the sentries at their posts and Trey on his bedroll in the brush near Amanda's window. Brantly and Lionel had much in common despite having been raised worlds apart in diverse cultures. They were both without mates, they were content with solitude. They placed high value on privacy. They had suffered losses of loved-ones; about which they did not speak. They simply carried their pain as part of who they were. They were honest and brave.

Lionel had been silently looking over the top of his glass at Brantly who seemed to be content in some distant place in his mind. Lionel said, "I want to be clear about something we have not discussed. I've given much thought to our endeavor and defer to your leadership. I mean to sell myself to you as a combatant. You've seen me shoot. I am an expert horseman. I know how to follow orders. I have a vested interest in our success. I've considered the risk and my responsibilities to Amanda. I will not charge for my service and I believe I will live up to my reputation as 'Sir Sniper'. I've discussed it with Amanda and she says, 'You go, Daddy. You go and get those sons of bitches.' That's my girl."

Brantly nodded once. "Excellent." They drained their glasses.

Lionel, once again topped their glasses, and said, "This may well be a flagrant violation of our respect for each other's privacy, however, we recognize that we are both bold and blunt in our manner of dealing with life. So with all due respect and willingness to accept your wrath at my taking a liberty inspired by good whiskey, I would like to know if there has ever been a significant woman in your life."

Lionel had over the years developed the ritual of enjoying an after dinner drink and settling in a chair with a book. Brantly would only on rare occasions have a whiskey or tequila. On this night, Lionel had kept their glasses full. Brantly had no sense of how much he'd consumed. His entire life had been lived in the heart of danger and adventure. The lives of many men had come to an end at the hands of Brantly Stormer. Indians, bandits, outlaws had closed their eyes for the last time as a result of his rigid sense of justice.

Marriage was never a wise option for a Texas Ranger. Carnal urges were satisfied by whores. For many years he had a meaningful, fraternal friendship with a talkative ranger named Tater Fuller. Tater was short for Potato, his favorite food. He had a fondness for whoring which rivaled his love for 'taters'. He was a good story teller and could go on for hours about whores he'd known. Brantly would listen in silence with an occasional nod and grunt. Tater was a valiant fighter, a menacing pistolero with a golden heart, a quick smile and a big laugh. He was killed in an Indian fight and left Brantly mute with grief. He never stopped thinking about the things he wished he'd taken the time to share with Tater.

Brantly thought it odd that his first reaction to Lionel's question was Tater coming to mind. This was a rare opportunity. Lionel was unlike any other man Brantly had ever known. He had absolute trust in the man. They were alone. He knew there would be no judgement. He reached for his glass and took a sip of whiskey. "Her name was Annie." He closed his eyes and watched her float in the darkness there.

He went back to a time just before he left home to join the Texas Rangers. It was a hoedown. Music, dancing, a gathering of local folks, settlers, farmers and ranchers. Annie stood with her mother watching the dancing. It seemed to Brantly that

forces of light in the sky had come together to
form a beam to shine down on Annie. Golden
shimmering curls the color of sunflowers moved in
the soft breeze. Her eyes bluer than a morning sky
were smiling with delight. Brantly could not move
his gaze from the sight. She was seventeen. He
was nineteen.

In a trance, he moved directly to her. He
nodded to her mother, removing his hat and asked
for permission to ask Annie to dance. He took her
delicate hand and led her to the dancers. As they
walked, a fragrance of new-mown hay came to
him. She floated in his arms as light as a cloud. He
was instantly convinced he'd never been happier.
"I lay awake all night thinking to give up
everything I'd ever thought about doing. I'd marry
Annie, we'd have children and live happily ever
after."

The next morning, he got up in the dark,
saddled his horse and rode to the nearest Ranger
camp and signed the papers. The Captain
immediately sent him with four other rangers on a
mission to rescue what remained of a settler family
captured by a small group of young Comanche
warriors. Brantly killed three of them and the
rangers were able to bring back two of the women.
A mother and her child. A week later he was sent
on another mission and then another. Each night

since he joined the Rangers, he would close his eyes and see Annie glowing. He knew that he'd done the right thing for both of them but could not stop thinking about her and how totally different his life would be had he followed the impulse to marry her. Six months flew by when he got word that Annie had married a young rancher and moved to Nebraska.

"I still think about her...after all the years...and try to imagine what her life is like." It was the very first time he'd ever spoken about Annie to anyone. It felt good to tell about her and hint at how lasting the feelings about her still were.

Lionel raised his glass saying, "It's a great story. Tells so much about you. Thank you for sharing it with me."

Brantly nodded and grinned his tight lopsided grin.

♣

Brantly and Juanito had made their way through the tunnel to the trap door and the grain bin. They found that there were two men on duty in the barn at night, Alejandro and Domingo. One slept on a cot in a vacant stall while the other was meant to be awake and on guard. They were the only discernable obstacles at night in the barn.

Armed guards were posted on the walls surrounding the courtyard and on the roof of the hacienda. A fountain, long unused for want of repair, was planted with an array of flowers just below the balcony where Rojas appeared with his morning coffee. He could look across at an arena where Sergio and one of his caballeros worked horses.

Often Rojas was awake in the middle of the night. He would take advantage of his restlessness and moved silently out to the walls or roof to check on the vigilance of the guards. On the occasion of catching one snoring, he flung him off the roof twenty-five feet to the hard ground. When he regained consciousness, he was offered the choice of leaving or staying awake on the job. The discovery of a broken arm disqualified him as an armed guard. Rojas was vexed at his reckless temper and the resultant loss of a guard, incompetent though he was. He put his boot in the man's ass as he kicked him out the gate cussing his birth every step of the way.

Encarnita was not possessed of the timid, submissive, demeanor typical of most peasant Mexican women. The conflict with Rojas did not end with her being knocked unconscious. She recovered quickly enough to go at him again. He unleashed a series of battering blows that left in bed in a separate room for days. Her face had turned to swollen purple pulp. Her relationship with Rojas was based completely on what he provided for her. She knew very well that he was unpredictable, volatile and capable of extreme violence. He had never beaten her to the extent that he just had. A venomous loathing began to grow inside her as she lay in pain on the bed barely able to change her position. He had no interest in seeing her and left her in the care of a servant woman.

# 13

The wagon was loaded with more dynamite, bombs and sticks designed to be thrown and explode. Stick Comstock would drive the team of very fast horses. Juanito knew where the bombs should be placed for maximum effect. He would ride shotgun and kill everyone he could on their mad charge into the compound and courtyard. The snipers were to kill all the guards simultaneously as Trey and Brantly made their way through the tunnel to the barn. They would capture and disable the two stable hands who were only employed peasants. Trey would take the stallion, Zarco, bareback and escape at blinding speed right out the front gate to the narrow pass through the rock. Once through, the planted dynamite would blow the rock apart and seal the pass. Any pursuers would end in a rocky grave. The tunnel would explode at the same time, trapping bandits seeking escape.

♣

Bottles and tin cans hung from trees moving in the breeze. Various targets made of straw-stuffed sacks with faces painted on heads bunched and tied were partially hidden among trees. Brantly watched with his pocket watch in hand as each man took his turn. Peyton, Digger, Juanito, Mathew Brawls, Taggert, Lionel, Stick, Trey, Clayton, each on a signal from Brantly, had to run the course as fast as possible, shooting the weapon of his choice, and hit as many targets as he could. Brantly would be the last to go.

Then they had to do it horseback. Then they had to do it again…and again. Then Trey went to the training arena where Amanda had several horses haltered, all without saddles. He practiced mounting them bareback from the ground and galloping off. Then she put a horse on a 25 foot longe line so it could gallop around her in a 50-foot circle without guidance from the rider. She made him ride with his hands on his head, with his arms folded across his chest, twisting from the waist, left and right, then reach down and touch his left foot with his right hand, then his right foot with his left hand. Then reverse, going clockwise doing the same things. Trey worked for hours until Amanda said, "All rightie ho. I think you're ready for the circus. Bloody well done, Ol' Chap."

Trey sat on the sweaty back huffin' and puffin', "Thanks."

*Alex Cord*

She smiled up at him and touched his knee. "I believe you can ride anything with hair on it."

"I am ready."

♣

Brantly called them all together in the bunkhouse. "Day after tomorrow we'll have a full moon. We'll attack at midnight. We'll hit 'em like a twister, with less warning and more destruction. We're ready, and we've got two more days to hone our edge. They have never had to face anything like us." He gazed around the room pausing to lock eyes with each man for a few silent seconds. In the depth of his cold gray eyes lay a hint of mirth. "Let's get some sleep and an early start."

# 14

Jesus and Valentina Galindo were moved from their humble abode to Lionel's ranch for the time of war. One of Lionel's hands was to see to their sheep and goats. The luxury of the ranch compared to their little adobe house was overwhelming. Lionel and Brantly assured them it was only for a few days at most and did all they could to make them feel at ease. Amanda welcomed them as long lost loved ones. The promise of how different life would be after the evil and fear that they'd lived under for so long had been destroyed, held out faint hope but was far too challenging for them to fully accept as true.

Each man was to carry his weapons of choice and abundant ammunition. The snipers, Lionel, Peyton, Taggert, and Digger had their respective long guns. Mathew Brawls armed with his heavy knife, a pistol and a lever-action Winchester would be on the wagon loaded with dynamite bombs. Stick would drive the team of well-trained, horses that could outrun the wind. Juanito had his pistol and a knife.

Every part of their plan had to occur simultaneously. Their success depended on the overwhelming boldness of their attack.

The sun descended leaving an orange and purple glow along the western horizon. The men watched as it faded and vanished. Like a huge black cloak, the dark of night arrived. Stars and the moon waited in the wings. Brantly, Trey and Clayton made their silent way to the place next to the narrow pass below the entrance to the tunnel. Buck Taylor, one of Lionel's trusted hands was along to stay with the horses a distance away to allow for the explosions.

The snipers crawled up the steep hillsides through mesquite and chaparral to their vantage posts looking across to the walls and roofs of Hacienda del Diablo. It was a black, cloudy night. It was impossible to see clearly the guards on the walls and roofs. The snipers knew they had time. They remained calm and confident as they waited.

Brantly and Trey crawled into the tunnel and lit their lamp. Clayton remained behind with a lamp to be lit to signal the snipers. Clayton checked his watch. It was close to midnight. As if in accordance to a contract with God, the moon appeared in a sea of stars. Brantly and Trey crept through the grain into the barn and rendered the guard on duty unconscious. While Trey went to the stall where Zarco stood, Brantly eased into the stall where the other guard slept and knocked him in the head with his pistol. These men were not banditos but hard-working peasants.

Clayton signaled the snipers and gunfire began. A bandito charged into the barn as Trey came out of the stall riding Zarco. The bandito raised his gun, Brantly shot him dead and ran to the exit to clear the way for Trey who came at a gallop toward the front gate. It was shut with a guard struggling with his gun trying to make sense of what was occurring as men fell from the walls and roofs. Brantly shot the gate guard as Trey galloped toward the shut gate and soared over it. Several Comancheros had staggered out of beds in a daze and fired at the fleeing horse and rider. Brantly killed all of them.

At the sounds of the first shots, Stick stirred up his team and raced off down the narrow trail toward the hacienda. Trey and Zarco came right toward them burnin the breeze. They passed each other at full speed. Gunfire had not abated as they approached the now open gate and charged into the courtyard. Comancheros were appearing from everywhere. Brantly had opened the gate and was shooting every bandito as they appeared.

Rojas had staggered out of bed in complete shock. He grabbed a bedside rifle and moved out to his balcony. Encarnita had recovered enough to get out of bed. The hate in her continued to fester as she looked at herself in a mirror and saw that her face had suffered permanent damage. She would never look the same again. Rojas had never come to see her and the destruction he had done. She quietly entered his bedroom and seeing him on the balcony moved quickly up behind him as he had raised his rifle and was taking aim at Juanito carrying explosives toward the house. In one swift move with the force of her weight behind it, she plunged an eight-inch kitchen knife into his back to the hilt, below his ribs. His gun fired into the sky as his back arched and she shoved him over the railing to the chaos below.

Pure instinct had caused Juanito to look up and see what had happened. A bandito was running out of the hacienda as Mathew was entering with a keg bomb filled with nails. He shoved it into the man's chest, drew his big knife and severed his neck to where only a few strands of tissue kept his head from falling to the ground. Stick was busy with wires and detonators. The entire place swarmed with renegades, banditos, Comancheros, all dazed, milling about, shooting aimlessly. The snipers had made their way down from the hills in time to overpower the Devils disciples and send them hopping over coals in hell.

The courtyard was a carpet of corpses. Juanito had gone through the house and found Encarnita and a few servants and brought them out. Clayton rode up to say that several banditos had found their way into the tunnel and were about to escape. "Just banditos, no peasants?" Brantly asked.

"Far as we know."

"Blow the tunnel."

Clayton nodded and rode away. Brantly and his men went through the hacienda and then the barns and bunkhouses. The sun began a slow rising on a golden day. They found the pretty mare and several other fine horses.

Brantly and Lionel determined to take the horses to Lionel's ranch and figure it out from there. They stood in the courtyard looking at the death and destruction. Brantly took off his hat and ran his fingers through his hair. He rubbed his face. The sound of the tunnel explosion shook the ground where they stood. "Now we must destroy *the house of the devil*. Interesting, he named it exactly what it is."

Stick was pleased with the placement of his bombs and warned everyone to stand clear. "There really was no rush was there?"

"I guess I underestimated how good we are." Brantly seemed to be off somewhere as he spoke. Lionel was watching him closely. He was always very curious about Brantly and what his feelings and thoughts were. They were now part of a monumental event.

They were all stunned by what had occurred. Brantly scanned the area and saw no movement among the bodies strewn over the courtyard. He turned his eyes to the sky then back down to the scene before him. "Here we are, the sun is up, it's a beautiful morning...and none of these folks is gonna get to live it."

"And they don't deserve to." Lionel stated.

"Aint that the truth. Killin' men in the morning is somber work." Brantly looked over at Stick waiting at attention. "Stick, are you ready?"

"Waitin on you, sir."

"Everybody clear?"

"Yes, sir."

Brantly took one last look. "Do it."

The explosion was immense. It blew most of the roof off the building, walls collapsed, doors and furniture flew through the air midst a world of swirling dust, adobe bricks and plaster. It seemed an eternity for all to settle. Scattered witnesses stood slack-faced in awe. Finally, the air cleared revealing the huge heap of rubble that was *the house of the devil.* Encarnita stood next to Juanito. Household staff and other peasant workers huddled together in disbelief. A silence hovered like a shroud. Suddenly, it was broken by a booming laugh that grew in intensity and volume. Stick stood in the middle of the wreckage with his back arched and roaring with laughter at the sky. Unknown to Stick, beneath his feet lay a length of beam. Under the beam, covered with debris were the shoulders of Manuel Rojas, face down with the handle of the knife sticking out of his back.

# 15

The poor peasant workers had wandered back to the humble places they'd left to serve at the hacienda where they were fed and could earn enough to help their families survive.

Juanito was guiding Brantly and Lionel through the wreckage of the house. He showed them what remained of the ingenious secret passages that his father had constructed. They moved with caution through the debris to avoid turning an ankle. Juanito stopped to look down through broken wood and ashes at something that caught his attention. He bent and dug carefully with his bare hand. After a few minutes of probing he pulled out a silver chalice. He held it up and blew off the dust and dirt. It had one small dent. Brantly turned to see as Juanito held it out to him. Lionel joined them. "Good Lord. That is a beautiful chalice."

"It is from the church of my people. I have seen it many times." Juanito went to the spot where he found it and began to carefully remove pieces of debris and put them aside. He found part of a wooden chest and a piece with a hinge attached. Lionel put the chalice in a safe place and joined Juanito. Brantly was already there. They quickly became a team as they eagerly dug through the trash uncovering first a silver candle stick, then another, and another chalice. They soon realized there were coins and jewelry scattered over a much larger area than first thought.

The dynamite had revealed Rojas's treasure chest of plunders taken by force from innocent victims.

♣

Amanda had been waiting at the entrance gate with Valentina and Jesus since an hour before midnight. Amanda paced like a caged tiger while Valentina and Jesus stood quietly. She wondered if it would be possible in the silent night to hear any sound of gunfire. She speculated aloud with herself and concluded that they were too far away. Valentina remained stoically silent as midnight arrived and the clock ticked on. In the dead quiet of the unmoving night, Amanda stopped pacing and listened intently. Yes, she was sure she could hear the muted sound of a running horse. She quickly became certain as she moved away from the gate and down the path to the rest of the world.

Valentina and Jesus moved with her. They all could hear the hoof beats coming closer. Out of the soft gray light of the moon, the horse and rider emerged. He stopped beside her, slipped off the stallion and into her arms. She wanted more than two arms to embrace both Trey and Zarco. It had been a long run, dodging bullets for the early part, but they were unscathed and safe at home. When she did get her arms around Zarco's neck, though restless from the long run, he rumbled from deep within a snorting nicker of recognition. Her eyes filled with tears as he rested his chin on her shoulder. Valentina and Jesus moved close enough to touch Trey's shoulder. Amanda looked at him and whispered, "Thank you, Trey. What a heroic thing to have done. Thank you." Her tears kept spilling out as she put her arms around him and held him close.

They all walked through the gate and the waiting hands patting Trey on the back. Amanda opened the gate to the big turnout pen and led Zarco in. She took off the halter and lead rope that had served as a bridle, and turned him loose. He trotted off kicking his heels in the air, put his nose to the ground. He sunk to his knees and rolled luxuriously from one side to the other. They all hung on the top rail watching as he sprang to his feet, kicked at the sky and galloped off for a few strides, then relaxed into a trot. Good to be home.

# 16

Three days had passed since the midnight raid that had accomplished the impossible. Hordes of the devil's disciples had been 'bedded down' by a handful of soldiers of Christ. The evil dictator had been destroyed, his army decimated. And not a scratch on any of the good guys. There was much to be done. There was no one to lay claim to any of Rojas's assets.

Lionel, Brantly and Clayton put their heads together and decided that the livestock, cattle and horses, would be sold and the money gained distributed among the peasants who had been Rojas's victims. They moved without delay to see it done. Juanito saw to the dispersal of a few burros and mules among local farmers he knew. The pretty mare and a couple of other fine horses were brought to Lionel's ranch.

The mare was well-bred of Spanish Andalusian blood. She was a dark bay with a long mass of black mane and tail. Amanda stood in awe. "She's a perfect bride for Mr. Zarco."

Lionel put his arm around Amanda and said, "We've got to come up with a name for her."

It didn't take Amanda but an instant to say, "What do you think about naming her after Mother?"

That took him by surprise. "Camilla." He let it soak for a minute. "Zarco and Camilla." He turned to look at Amanda and went back for a moment in his mind to a time when Camilla was in his life. "Sounds good to me."

"Camilla," said Amanda as she reached up to stroke the mare's face. She shook her head, just to flaunt her mane.

Trey stepped forward. "Camilla, I like it."

♣

Brantly, Lionel, and Clayton made a few final tours of what had been Hacienda del Diablo to see and evaluate the results of their efforts. They concluded that as far as they could tell they had eliminated all of the villains. Of course they could not know about any relatives or sympathizers that might still exist and rise up, but at best it would take a long time for anyone to organize anything like what they had destroyed.

Before long the place was looted and abandoned to disintegrate and become a crumble in the desert.

Lionel decided it was time to celebrate. He and Amanda and Valentina organized a party. It became a huge event. Neighbors, Tom Hastings and wife, Susan, Senator Harley May and wife, Mattie were in attendance along with all the hands and their girlfriends and wives. Juanito had gathered musicians and relatives. The guests of honor were Brantly and his *soldiers of Christ*.

The food was a banquet for royalty of any sort. The music was spirited and filled with joy. Every one took advantage of the space for dancing. Brantly had for days been occupied with thoughts about Valentina. There'd been little opportunity for contact until now. She stood radiant there in the moonlight moving ever so slightly to the music. His mind leaped instantly back to the hoedown of his boyhood and Annie glowing golden as he asked her mother for permission to ask her to dance. Valentina was a shimmering vision of dark beauty. Brantly's heart began to race as he moved toward her. It was as if he'd never seen her before. Of course he had and had always thought she was attractive but he always had something else to cut off any further thinking about Valentina. He stopped in front of her and looked into her raven-black eyes and bowed slightly in a courtly fashion and said, "May I have this dance?"

She smiled up at him with a twinkle and said, "Si, señor."

He took her hand and she flowed into his arms. As they moved together to the music and his heart pounded, he thought, *my God, and for all these years...*

When the music stopped, Lionel stepped forward. "Ladies and gentlemen, I am very pleased to have been a part of something so much bigger and more important than I ever thought it would be. I would like you to meet some very special men who have changed the lives of many people in this part of the country. People who were oppressed and terrorized for years are now free, thanks to these men." He then proceeded to introduce each man. The most he could get from them was a nod, a tip of a hat, a small hand gesture; except for Stick who raised one finger in acknowledgment then threw his head back and unleashed his raucous laugh loud enough to stir life in a graveyard. "And last, our leader, the man who made it all happen, Brantly Stormer." Brantly was standing next to Valentina. He lifted his hand just a little and quickly dropped it.

Two days later the men were fixin to leave and go their separate ways. Brantly had gathered them all in the bunkhouse. "I'm not much at speechifying...but what y'all did was beyond words anyway. You know how big a deal it was. And by the grace of God we did not lose a drop of blood. I don't know that I will ever really understand how we did it. Each one of you is an amazing individual. I will be grateful till my last breath. It's been a privilege. Keep an eye peeled. There are still some scattered bands of Comanche warriors that are lurkin to offer unwanted haircuts. Sir Sniper wants to say something. I'm gonna take Jesus and Valentina back to their place. If I don't see you before you leave. Adios." He turned to go but stopped and looked back. "Oh I'm sure y'all will be keen to write to me so, I'll be lookin for your letters."

He stopped the wagon in front of the humble shelter and helped them get their things inside. One of Lionel's hands had camped there to look after Jesus's flock, so everything was in good shape. The old man was keen to see them. He took his stick and hobbled up the gentle slope behind the house. Brantly said, "shouldn't I go with him?"

"No, they are not far. He is getting around very well now. I know he would like to be alone with them. His sheep is the best medicine."

"He's one ole curly wolf."

"What that means?"

"Tough guy."

"Yes," she smiled, "he is curly wolf." They moved out the door to the front of the house where a chunk of log had been flattened into a crude bench. Brantly had come to realize that since the night of the party he was no longer the man he'd been for his entire life. An absolute transformation had occurred overnight. It was as if something had been growing inside of him for a long time without his knowledge. It had now reach maturity and was bursting forth. It was a wild, untamed thing over which he had no control.

He turned to face her and was surprised to know that he was not nervous or hesitant. It was as if another force had taken control. He did not touch her. The only contact between them was their eyes, unwavering. Her face was like a painting of a mystical being unconcerned with human issues. "I have an impossible thing to say. Feelings I've never had; words I've never spoken. Something unexpected is full inside of me. Like a tree that has grown and must be free to bloom." He suddenly burst into real laughter. Not a common Brantly trait. "It sounds like I'm trying to tell you, I'm pregnant. I'm not." He laughed again. "The truth is that I love you with all my heart and soul. I have never felt this before in my life. This is the first time I've ever spoken these words. I love you. I want to spend the rest of my life with you." He went on to tell her about the land on Lionel's ranch and that he would build a house that she and Jesus could come and live, and yes, the curly wolf could bring his flock. "I know this is mucho informacion, so just let it sink in and know that it comes from the deepest part of me. A part I didn't know existed."

"Are you asking me to marry you?"

"I am."

"My answer is, Si, Señor."

# 17

Mathew Brawls sat easily on his big Belgian-cross moving leisurely through the open prairie on his way back to where he'd come from. He was not a deep-thinking man. He had never married, had never had children, had mostly been a fighter. He did have an unswerving sense of justice. He was known as a righteous individual who would only sign on if he believed in the fight. He'd killed a lot of scalp hunters who preyed on innocent settlers trying to make new lives for their families. He felt good about most of what he'd done. In the solitude of his ride dwelt the opportunity for reflection. He'd had a little dog for years, a Queensland Heeler, a loyal critter who fawned on his every move. If he had to be away he'd leave her with a neighbor. They had formed a deep, meaningful bond and on occasion he'd turn down gainful employment if it meant too long away from Buckshot. She'd wandered off and got taken by a wolf just before Brantly had contacted him. Mathew probably would not have said yes to Brantly if Buckshot were still with him. One of the odd thoughts that occurred to him as he rocked along on his big horse was that he would look for a pup to raise.

The past weeks came back to him in small sections of memory. His heart had gone out to the plight of the peasants and at ease as he was with violence, this was the first time he felt an emotion about the task at hand. With it had come a never before sense of having done something honorable. He puffed up a bit. Then spat a wad of brown juice into the chaparral.

A feeling of sadness came upon him and mixed in his chest with the fading pride. He thought about his days of fighting, his main occupation, coming to a close. *Oh, there'll still be some killin to be done,* he thought, then spat again.

The prairie was hot, wide, and flat, as far as the eye could see. Two dark specs appeared in the great distance. Mathew immediately knew they were Comanche renegades just drifting like fisherman trolling. If he could see them, they could see him. Rather than deal with the uneasiness of trying to figure what they might do, he decided to try a deception. He angled off toward the east. The sun was fixin to set as a muted dusk hovered casting a palette of pastel hues. There were no trees but some thick sage and mesquite looked promising. He hobbled the big horse and built a small fire. Using his saddle, bedroll and brush stuffing, he managed to create the illusion of a man sleeping. He moved off with his buffalo gun and big knife and hunkered down in the dust. Well after dark descended as he lay absolutely motionless, one of the renegades damn near stepped on him. He took the man down and severed his windpipe without a sound. He focused the rifle on his horse and the dwindling fire. The half-breed appeared with a knife in hand and stooped over the sleeping dummy as Mathew Brawls blew most of his head off.

Mathew was actually able to get some sleep before sunrise. He decided to lead one horse and sure enough the other followed. He'd sell them or trade them on his way north to find a puppy.

Wild-eyed and scowling as if affronted, Stick got on the train and as it started to move off, he stuck his pale head out the window and yowled his outrageous laugh. Passengers inside were a little unsettled for a time.

Digger Carlson had taken a fancy to one of the finer geldings that were part of the spoils of war with Rojas. Knowing that the money would go to the victimized peasants, he purchased the horse and would ride it home. He'd come from up in the panhandle near Oklahoma. He stood by the horse admiring him and stroking his shining coat. He put his foot in the stirrup and eased up settling lightly in the saddle. With a gleam in his falcon eyes, he reached down for Brantly's hand and said, "Let's do it again sometime."

Brantly nodded his crooked smile and said, "Sometime…"

Digger turned his horse and rode away.

Taggert Kilman looking every inch, a gunfighter—it wasn't just his attire and guns but an aura of menace about the man—stood facing Brantly. He was the man who had threatened to kill Brantly, the man who would not shake anyone's hand. Looking straight into Brantly's eyes with a cold, unsmiling glare, he said, "I enjoyed it." He smiled, and offered his hand. They shook, he stepped onto his horse and rode through the gate at an easy lope.

Trey's baby brother, Peyton, decided to hire on for a while to help with the building of Brantly's house and maybe develop a relationship with his brother. "I can push a saw and swing a hammer."

It was unavoidable, Juanito had become a hero among his people. He would have much preferred to remain unknown but it was not to be. He found the priest who'd been whipped by Rojas and began to study with him. Juanito was destined to become a leader in their community. His cousin, Raul, became a close confidant and source of valuable information acquired from his frequent presence at the cockfights.

Each man had been paid the agreed upon 2,000 dollars plus a generous bonus from Sir Lionel. Building materials were gathered and being moved up to the 250 acres that were part of Brantly's fee. He was eager to get started.

Destiny isn't bound by rules and custom. No one would ever have predicted that Sir Lionel Lawson and Brantly Stormer would develop a friendship as close as brothers. They might've been twins separated at birth and raised at opposite ends of the earth to become mature men. Then destiny caused their paths to cross and discover who they are. Such was the bond that had grown between them. They were both men of deep thoughts and feelings but few words.

Once again, they were alone in Lionel's study. A palpable warmth seemed to emanate from the walls of books as if to impart the wisdom within. Brantly held the volume of Shakespeare's plays open to a random page as he moved his lips without sound.

Lionel poured whiskey into their glasses at the table and sat in the deep leather chair. Brantly closed Shakespeare and put him back on the shelf. He moved to the other chair and sat opposite Lionel. They raised their glasses to each other. Lionel said, "Cheers. Here's to your new house."

Brantly sipped his whiskey, licked his lips, smiled and said, "This ain't no coffin varnish." He took a deep breath and said, "I'm gonna marry Valentina."

Lionel took just a minute to let it sink in. "I think that would be a good thing." They both raised their glasses. "This is a damn fine way to pick up from where we left off last time. It was a little girl at a hoedown when you were just a nipper."

Brantly smiled at the memory. "Gonna have to build a room for her daddy, till the angels come for im."

"I don't know; old Jesus could end up doing a jig on your mound."

"I sure wouldn't put it past im."

"What decided you?"

"I didn't know. Just too dim-witted. It's like I just woke up knowing that I' ve loved her since the first time I looked at her. I just…I guess I just couldn't believe it. I didn't know I could feel that."

# 18

While the sands slipped through the glass, the house began to take shape with Peyton swinging a hammer and pushing a saw and brother Trey joining when he could. Brantly worked like a man possessed. He was eager to close the gaps between his times with Valentina. Sir Lionel had offered him the use of a guest room if he wanted to be married before the house was finished. However, old Jesus was not to be left alone at his humble abode. So the construction progressed at a feverish pace.

Juanito was a diligent student under the tutelage of Father Roberto who had become his mentor. There was much to learn in the ways of the church. It would require many months of serious study for Juanito to be invested with the authority of the clergy. In the meantime, he assisted Father Roberto in baptisms and weddings and refurbishing their church. For the first time in many years, the humble people of the little village were free to worship without the fear of being threatened, robbed and abused by Manuel Rojas and his band of cut-throats.

The last nail had been pounded in. The roof sealed. Jesus's sheep driven up to their new pastures. The wedding was planned by Valentina and Amanda. The ceremony was to be performed by Father Roberto assisted by Juanito Torres.

It was a small, dignified, gathering of ranch hands, neighbors and villagers from across the river. Father Roberto spoke eloquently of what it means to be married in the eyes of God. Brantly placed the ring on her finger and took her in his arms. He thought he might collapse with emotion when he bent to kiss her gently on full, soft, yielding lips. It was a sensation unknown, and mysterious to him.

Several weeks had gone by with Brantly continuing to work on their new home. Valentina—when not helping Brantly—had taken to joining Juanito in his village to help some of the local women with their children.

With the additional horses and cattle, there was plenty of work to occupy another hand, so Peyton stayed on to work with brother Trey. What with the building of Brantly's house and now the cattle and horses, he'd been putting in a lot of hours on the job without a break. He loosened the cinch and pulled the saddle from his horse's back and slung it on a rail. As he reached for the sweaty blanket, he said to Trey, "I'm fixin to have a bath and ride on over to Wolfpaw. Whyn't you come with me?"

"It's tempting…but…no. I think my days…or nights, at Wolfpaw are coming to an end."

Peyton shook his head in a pitying way. "Be that way."

Trey said, "You be careful."

♣

The bar at Wolfpaw was stacked with elbow to elbow patrons and a few whores in-between. Peyton was working on his second straight tequila with a beer chaser on the bar. Next to him were two men. One was a big raw-boned, pock-faced man with a five-day growth of hair surfacing the plum-colored pock pits. He swallowed a beer without taking a breath and reached for his whiskey. The other was a small ferret-like critter with the eyes of a rattler. He slung back a shot of tequila. The bartender came by to refill their glasses. Pock face leaned forward, "You know of a man named Brantly Stormer?"

"Why?" He filled the glasses.

"Oh, he's an old pardner from way back. Haven't seen im in years. Like to visit with im. Heard he's around these parts."

"I've heard the name from somewhere. But that's about it. Don't know anything about him." He moved over to Peyton. "Want anothern?"

Peyton shook his head, put some money on the bar, and turned and left.

## About Alex Cord

ALEX CORD

Alex Cord is an American actor who is best known for his portrayal of Michael Coldsmith Briggs III, better known as Archangel, in fifty-five episodes of the CBS adventure television series Airwolf.

## Praise for Alex Cord

"...I felt a real affinity with the characters and hope to see this book as a motion picture."
**HARRISON FORD, Actor**

"Writers, said Anthony Burgess, must know about things as well as words. Alex Cord knows about cutting horses, love for a woman, and the long shadow cast by the headstone of a lost son. These he tells about with true feeling."
THOMAS McINTYRE, Author, Seasons of Days: A Hunting Life

"Alex has written one of the finest love stories I've ever read. It's sure to make a great movie."
ERNEST BORGNINE, Academy Award-winning Actor

"Alex is an excellent horseman, an excellent actor, and as expected has come up with an excellent book."
SYLVESTER STALLONE, Actor, Writer

CORD's award-winning second book 'A FEATHER IN THE RAIN' is currently heading towards its destiny as a Hollywood movie. CORD's new book "THE MAN WHO WOULD BE GOD" has just been released and you will love it.

Made in the USA
Las Vegas, NV
13 January 2021

15705218R00075